Saved
By Grace

The Untrue Story of Joe Allen

James A. Moore III

Outskirts Press, Inc.
Denver, Colorado

Saved by Grace
The Untrue Story of Joe Allen

Outskirts Press
http://www.outskirtspress.com

ISBN-10: 1-4327-0308-0
ISBN-13: 978-1-4327-0308-0

Printed in the United States of America

Dedication

Table of Contents

Part One:
Boyhood
and
Young Man

Chapter 1
Boyhood

Joe Allen was born on June 1, 1978 in Ivy ,South Carolina. His dad was a local teacher and coach at the high school. His mom was the athletic secretary. His sister Lauren was 5, they were the only kids his parents had. His parents were Christians, and they attended church. They were a good religious family and tried to do right and do good stuff.

Joe was born to Jack and Joey Allen. Jack had been born in Arizona in 1945 and was one of 4 kids. There was 3 boys and 1 girl, she the youngest. Jack was the youngest boy. They moved around the southwest for 10 years and finally settled in South Carolina in 1957. He was a popular student with all the guys. He had a few girlfriends, but sports kept him very much busy. He slept with a few girls to make his reputation in the locker room good. He drank beer with the guys as well.

His parents became Christians when he was 15. They told him he needed Jesus as well but he acted wild at times. He went to church and acted good some. Finally, he accepted Jesus on his graduation day and hung out with Christians that summer. In college, he hung out with Christians.

He always enjoyed sports and enjoyed playing. He played some in college but an injury made him quit. The coach liked him and made him a trainer/assistant. He enjoyed coaching and teaching and stayed in South Carolina. He accepted the job at Ivy Middle School in 1971 and became the Junior High basketball coach and history teacher. It is here he met the secretary, Joey Brown.

Joey had always lived in Lansing, South Carolina. She was born in 1942, and had 2 brothers who were 4 and 2 years older than her. Her sister was born in 1946. She was part of a very close family, and they loved each other very much. They all promised to live close to each other always. And they always would live in the Southeast, many in Carolinas or Georgia.

Her dad, Grant Hillman, was a pastor at Lansing Baptist Church from 1941-1978. He was very much loved. Joey believed in God, and was saved, and as a girl she wanted to follow Jesus always. As a teen, she strayed some, and slept with a few guys. Her parents found out, and gave her tough love. She started living as a Christian again.

She went to college in Georgia and strayed some again. She married at 19 and was divorced a year and a half later. She finished college in Georgia in 1966. She worked in Lansing for 2 years as a k-5 teacher. She then accepted a job at Ivy Middle School, 2 hours from Lansing. She was the secretary for the principal. She was there for 3 years, and dated a few men who did not work out. And then Jack came.

Jack and Joey dated a few times starting in October, and fell in love. In February, she found out she was a month pregnant, and they eloped, and neither one's parents nor families were very happy. Her brothers threatened to beat him up. They finally accepted facts when Jack and Joey had a "real wedding" for all in June 1972. Lauren was born in early October. Joey took that school year off with the baby, before returning in Fall 73. She has a close friend who could not have kids to watch the baby.

Joe was named after his mom. His parents had planned on 2 kids, hopefully a boy and girl. Jack made sure Joe would be the last kid. He was a happy baby. The families got together a lot. All of Joey's family lived either in Lansing or Ivy. Most of Jack's family was in the Carolina's, but his sister lived in Georgia. Joe was a smart baby and was quick to learn to crawl, talk, and walk. He could read a little at age 3. He was the smartest kid in preschool. He was very active with the other kids. Other kids were shy at 1st, but not Joe. All the other kids wanted to play with him. He had very good manners, and was not selfish, as he always shared all the toys. He was a very quick learner, and impressed all the teachers. At times, he was even teaching the 5 and 6 year olds new things, and he was only 3.

And then, they moved. When he was 4, his dad accepted a job as an Athletic Director/ coach/ Asst Principal at Lansing middle school. They lived with his mom's parents for 2 years. Joe loved being with his grandparents and seeing his cousins a lot. They were living in the house Joey had grown up in. Her parents had bought the house in 1940 and never wanted to move. (They would live there for over 50 years.) 3 of the 4 siblings and their families were living there. Only Joey's brother Kevin lived in Ivy, and that was always real close by.

Joe attended kindergarten in Lansing for 2 years. His sister Lauren was in elementary school, and was getting the highest marks in her grade. Both Allen kids were very smart. Again, Joe's teachers were very impressed. He taught the older kids at West Lansing Elementary School. His mom taught the 2nd grade, and she was right there at the school. Joe started putting on drama skits and telling funny jokes. His dad would get joke books from the library, and Joe would memorize them and repeat them. He always had a big crowd around him at recess. Even the teachers loved his jokes and funny stories he would tell of his family or of other people he would read about. He would always change the stories to make it look like they happened to him and to his family. He played sports at recess and gym and was a good athlete. He started reading well and would walk around classroom and help kids learn ABCS. All the teachers said he was going to be a good teacher or counselor one day. All the kids looked up to him. Despite young ages, kids would ask him for advice. He was also very popular in Sunday school, when his parents attended his grandpa's old church. Despite being retired, the whole family went every Sunday and it was a good church.

Joe and Lauren were close. They had fun contests, trying to outdo each other. Lauren could be just as gross as any one, even most guys. They played the funnest games. They played with her dolls and his army men. She would sleep in his room sometimes on bottom bunk. They watched Braves games together and cheered for Dale Murphy and Bob Horner. The Braves were good in 1982 and 1983, and were bad for a few years. They still cheered. They could play hide and go seek for hours and had unique hiding places. They played with Joe and Midge, another brother and sister in the neighborhood. They would play board games for a long time, and trivia games. They were both smart. They were best friends. They loved hide and go seek. Sometimes they used bad words, and giggled. They pretended to be famous preachers, singers, and movie stars. They always wore outrageous costumes. They picked on each other at times. But they stuck up for each other and would not let anyone else pick on the other one. She taught him to read. They drank a lot of coke, until their mom made them drink less. They also loved ice cream and watermelon. They wore the most outrageous costumes. They made up their own radio programs and played DJ and talk show host. They made up their own TV shows and interviewed each other and pretended to be TV stars. They pretended to be rich famous awesome athletes and they were the best ever. They would go around speaking and pretend to be famous TV evangelists. They took crazy wild pictures of each other in wildest situations. They would pretend the president was coming over and would clean the house. They would rearrange the bedrooms and make it cool. They would listen to music and

4

dance to it. They loved to watch TV shows, especially cartoons. They loved Christian shows. They would love spending a few nights at relatives, grandparents and cousins. They would help each other in school and life and advice. They would get each other little presents. She "went out" and the boys. And he "went out' and kissed the girls. They were best friends, and their parents were very happy. This was the case all in their childhood, no matter where they lived. They would watch out for each other always.

They had fun contests, trying to outdo each other. Lauren could be just as gross as any one, even most guys. Now, their parents did teach them good manners and how to do right. They acted well in public.

The families ate Sunday lunch together every other Sunday and rotated who hosted. They had good times. Joe wanted to stay there forever.

However, they only stayed in Lansing for 2 years. In March, his dad accepted a job as a dean of students and varsity basketball coach in Carters, North Carolina. They would move in July to prepare for the next school year. His parents were excited. Carters High School basketball team had only won 11 games in 7 seasons, and needed a good coach. Jack won 32 games and 2 championships coaching JV basketball in his 2 years in Lansing. It was a good program, but he decided he wanted a good challenge.

Joe resisted to the move a lot at first. He cried, he refused to listen to his parents, he left his room a mess, and he was mean to his sister and younger cousins. He would sass adults. He would be punished, but always say he did not care. His parents tried everything. He was acting up in school, and pushing friends away. He did not want to leave his friends, and wanted them mad at him so they would not miss him. All the kids did not understand what had happened to their best friend. They were upset.

Grandpa Hillman sat him down in early April and they had a long talk and then walk together. He showed him love and how to act. His Papa was one of his heroes.

Papa said "Joe, you are not acting right now. You need to start obeying your parents and start being nice to people again. You are not being a nice boy. I know you are sad about leaving, but this is what your mom and dad are doing, and you need to be happy."

"But Papa, I am going to miss y'all so much. I am so close to your house and all the family lives so close we can walk to the houses. I am going to live 3 hours away."

Grandpa said, "I know, Joe. But you will still see us. Sure, you won't see us as much. But we will still get together. And I know you will miss your friends here, but you will make many more new friends. You will meet many nice children. You will play sports, you like sports. You are a smart kid, and you know you are very nice and popular. And you can visit these friends here when you visit us. And one day you will be very happy you moved and you will have so many friends you won't want to leave them either. And act better to your friends, or you will never see them again. They are good friends. You don't want to ruin your last days here, you want everyone to be happy and remember good things about you."

Joe trusted his grandpa because he loved him so much. He had great respect for him. "Ok, grandpa. I believe you. I am sorry I haven't been acting well. I will do better."

Joe apologized to everyone, and was back to being Joe again. Everyone was happy he was nice. He enjoyed his last days there. He spent time with his friends and played with them a lot. When Joe turned 6 in early June, they had a big birthday party/ going away party.

The whole family got together in mid June and packed up all the family's stuff. They packed up and left. The family had a huge dinner party and some friends came over. It was at the Baptist church. Around 60 people came and wished them goodbye. The family moved to North Carolina.

They stayed there for 6 years. Joe was 6 years old when they moved, and spend his elementary school days there. Joe was shy at first being the new guy at school. But he became outgoing, brave, and would take almost any dare. He became popular. All the girls thought he was cute, and he had several "girlfriends." All the guys considered him their best friend. He would do cool things.

The teacher asked the students and him to stop with the dares in the 3rd grade, and they only did them at homes, and not in public. They were getting into too much trouble, and they felt it was not worth it. A couple of times, he even broke bones jumping out of trees. He was banned from the pool for the rest of the summer in 1986 for skinny dipping. He used the girl's bathroom once. He ate anything living people dared him to eat, even worms and bugs. He hung around his sister and her friends in his underwear. He did crazy things. His teachers and parents talked to him about doing stuff.

His dad said "Son, we do not go into the girl's bathroom. We do not see other people, especially boys and girls seeing each other without clothes. Skinny-dipping is not good. Eating bugs is not good. Accepting all these dares is not good for you. You are getting older now. You are going to be a big boy soon. We need to stop with the little kid stuff and grow up. You are a smart kid, and you need to mature some. You can still have lots of fun, but you will be in trouble if you don't grow up more."

Joe promised his dad he would act better. He wanted people not to think he was immature and did not want to be popular just for doing stupid stuff.

He matured some. He learned to calm down, he did not like being spanked or being grounded, he liked TV too much and playing with his friends. The dares decreased in the 3rd grade and stopped all together on the 4th grade in 1987. He was 9 years old now, and was acting more mature. His best male friends were Madison, Brian, Josh, and Jeremy. They would have sleepovers. He would write funny stories for all. He would watch TV shows and act out what he had seen. His favorites were Little House on the Prairie and Facts of Life. He loved the Little House books and Narnia, and would read the stories in a really dramatic voice for the kids. All the kids again turned to him for advice. He made the best grades in the school. He had chances to skip grades, but chose not to. He wanted a normal life, and loved his friends. He did help older kids with advice and school work. His sister and all her friends would ask him for help. And his sister was smart too. She played basketball and volleyball and made A's and B's. But Joe made all A's and was the most popular boy in the whole school.

Joe was also good at memorizing the Bible. He was great in Sunday school and church activities. He got a few patches for Bible memory and catechism. The church kids also looked up to him. A lot of them attended school with him as well. All the teachers wanted to teach him.

Joe also played sports, like his dad, and how he coached. He got a basketball hoop for his driveway when he was 8. He refused to lower it, even when the other kids had their goals lowered. He said he wanted to know how to shoot in a real goal early, and was not going to cheat. There was a park nearby, and some fields to play soccer, baseball, and flag football. Joe was excelling in sports early. He won a lot of medals for his speed and athleticism. All the coaches liked him and he won some coach's awards. His dad helped coach the YMCA basketball team so Joe could be on his team. Joe loved that. Jack was his hero. Joe scored a lot of soccer goals, and then felt selfish. He started passing more. He led the YMCA team in assists in basketball 4 years in a row. He out homered everyone in baseball all 6 years he lived there. He practiced a lot, and helped others. He helped many kids, boys and girls, get better in sports. As in helping in school work, he was very patient Many kids got better in sports due to his help.

He was an all around good guy. People called him an angel and a saint, which embarrassed him. He called himself a Christian, and memorized Bible, and went to church, but he did not believe all the stuff, and sometimes went along for show, and because he was supposed to. But he did enjoy it at times. He prayed and read his Bible (not for memorizing) a few times a week.

He kissed a few girls. He danced with them at the fun dances. He was in the 6th grade, junior high, at his 1st school dances. The girls were lined up to dance with him. He always danced with all the girls he could dance with. He even danced with some high schoolers some. He did make out with a few girls. But, he was always a gentleman. He would buy his dates gifts, and walk them to the door, and treated them like queens. They respected him because he showed them a lot of respect. He was only wild a few times, and that was making out with 3 girls. He was a good dancer. He loved the costume balls the most. He would pick out the craziest funniest costumes and dance funny. He always also wore the craziest Halloween costumes and went to all the houses. Everyone, of course, wanted to go with him trick or treating. The church had a good Reformation Day parties. It was their way of celebrating. People would dress up like Biblical characters. Joe always won the best costume.

His best female friends were Stephanie, Emily, Brittany, Laura, and Melody. He would save dances for them. They liked sports and would play ball games with the guys. Joe considered them as one of the guys. Except at dances and sometimes when he would kiss them.

Joe also won a lot of awards in school. He was always the teacher's pet. He would watch the class when they stepped out. As funny as he was, and with his skits, those were serious times, and the teachers respected and trusted him. And since the students respected Joe and looked up to him, they did not misbehave. Joe was a mature leader in the 5th and 6th grade. He was now among the older kids in school. Because his birthday was in the summer, he was one of 5 youngest kids in his grade, and the next to youngest boy. And yet, everyone looked up to him. He chose the activities and the games. People asked him for advice and help. He was considered very good in helping others and giving advice. He wrote an advice column and wrote cartoons for the school paper. He was a good artist, and liked writing cartoons. They were very funny and had some of the most original and unique characters. He would write storylines, and people would always read the cartoons to see what would happen to the animals next. His

9

animals were very strangely drawn.

Joe learned to play the piano. He collected audio tapes, records, and CDs. He would tape songs and Adventure in Odyssey programs for car trips and help the time go by quicker. Joe loved music. He loved country music, and was teased. He liked Christian contemporary music, some rock, MC Hammer, and loved listening to music as he relaxed, played hoops, and walked. He listed to Odyssey every Saturday; he thought Mr. Whitaker was cool.

Joe had become involved in drama as well. He was in the church musicals. He was in a few school plays and musicals. Everyone told him he was a good actor. He had been acting for years. His best friends and him would always star in the plays. He wrote funny stories about people and gave them to them. He was always the center of attention no matter what he did. He would gather crowds for his performances, skits, stories, and jokes. All the teachers wanted him to be a teacher, speaker, or preacher one day. He would seek out kids who didn't have any friends; some people called nerds and losers, and eat with them. Other kids would come, because it was Joe. The kid's self esteem would go up. Joe had no enemies; everyone wanted to be his friend. He would take time out to encourage kids in things he would say. He would write encouragement notes and seek out kids who were looking sad/upset and try to cheer them up. He would tell the kids he was praying for them. He would write funny notes and stories to the sad kids. He really helped them a lot.

Joe liked some TV shows. He liked watching the Atlanta Braves games. They were terrible in the late 80's, and Dale Murphy was not a very good player anymore, but they were the only team in the southeast at the time. Joe loved playing baseball. North Carolina had a new NBA team in the Hornets, and Joe would watch the team. Joe liked minor league games. He would love to see his dad coach the teams at the high school. He became friends with all the players. On the weekend road games, he would love traveling with the team and riding with them on the bus. They loved his stories and jokes as well. He loved the fellowship. He played on the 6th grade team, and was a good player. The team made him co-captain. He led the teams in a lot of stats.

He lifted weights at the YMCA and walked daily.

Joe went to church a lot, and tried to be a Christian at times. He did not understand everything. Some things confused him. He acted good and wanted to be good to please his family and not disappoint them. He believed in God, and prayed to accept Jesus at age 6. He memorized Bible. But he felt it was just for show, to show off. He did not want to disappoint them ever. He acted like a Christian a lot for his family. Sometimes he cussed however, and wanted to do bad things. He had stopped doing the dares, but still he felt a rebellious streak at times. But he contained himself and acted well so his family and friends and teachers would think he was a model kid. He always made good grades. He was naturally smart, but wanted to show off. And he did know God loved him always. And he knew he should be nice.

The families got together 6 times a year especially at holidays. They always had good fun times together. They remained close. His dad's brothers moved to Carters for a while. They always enjoyed seeing each other. They had good fun, fellowship, family time. They would get good games and play, and share memories, and take lots of pictures and video record. Joe loved photos, and had an entire album full of photos of family and friends. Joe and Lauren would play the piano for the family and do skits and sing.

Joe and Lauren had learned well from their parents. They may act crazy and wild at home, and gross each other and their mom out. But they could only be like that alone at home. Being with others was different. But they had great manners in public. They acted good at other people's houses and at restaurants. They did not talk to strangers and excelled. They were polite. Joe stood up for women. They obeyed their parents and spoke respectfully to everyone, especially adults. They did not fight others and solved differences. When they were real little kids, their mom and dad would take them to

11

restaurants and show them how to eat and treat others. They would have company over and Joe and Lauren would help serve. They did chores and helped set the table and wash the dishes and fold towels. They swept, mopped, and vacuumed. They were taught to clean the bathrooms and keep their rooms clean.

They always knew a good work ethic. Neither one had enemies. Everyone loved them. People agreed they had great parents. They were very mature.

Joe was taught respect for women by his dad, and he would mostly always remember this and treat women great. Like in the Bible, in Timothy, he would treat older women like his mom or grandma and younger women like sisters, and showed ultimate respect.

Joe and Lauren had to read and write and walk some every day and not watch too much TV. They did enjoy TV and had cable, but not too much, and only good clean TV shows and movies. They would rent movies from video store every weekend. They had 3 TVs and 2 VCRs. In 1988, they got a Nintendo. Of course, they would later get the cooler game systems. They loved Nintendo games and playing them. They loved to read, and they loved the Boxcar Children, Ramona Quimby and Encyclopedia Brown books. She loved the Sweet Valley Middle books and Joe loved them as well. He would never admit it to his friends though. They loved Disney movies, especially from the 60's and 70's. They loved Growing Pains, Facts of Life, Little House on the Prairie, Mama's Family, The Brady Bunch, Andy Griffith Show, Dennis the Menace, Mister Ed, and Full House were their favorite shows. Soon, they loved Family Matters and Steve Urkel was the man to them. They loved making fun of Saved by the Bell and always picked on it and found flaws. They liked watching soap operas and would make fun of them and act stuff out until their mom made them quit watching them.

He loved when his sister would have friends over, since they were older. He would spy on them and work out and flex and show off his muscles with no shirt and wait on them and do cute things. They all thought he was cute and hug and kiss them. He would love that. Lauren would tell him and them to stop. She told her friends he was just enjoying all the attention and they were just encouraging him and he would continue to do it. His parents thought it was great. They did tell him he always needed to wear shorts and close the door to the bathroom when he used it, after he had done a few things he shouldn't. Finally, he started going to friend's homes and spend the night when friends were over, especially sleep overs.

Joe really started to pay attention when Lauren started dating. He would make sure any prospective boyfriend would treat her with respect. He made sure they believed in God and went to church. He was glad his dad laid out some rules and a curfew. Joe would even say this stuff to big time athletes and strong guys. All the guys liked him as well. Some of Lauren's boyfriends would come over and play ball with him as long as Lauren did not mind. He liked a lot of her male friends. He would pretend to be the dad when he told the guys to treat Lauren right and to always respect her.

They fell in love with Showbiz Pizza and later Chuck E Cheeses. They would go there every Friday night. Joe loved the shows when the characters sang. They had birthday parties there. Joe loved the games, especially the bowling game. It was his favorite place, and they went there no matter where they moved to. Joe also loved to bowl and skate. He fished at local lakes and creeks, and always made good catches. He would hold hands with girls and they skated together. Joe had lots of fun doing all kinds of good stuff. He was never bored and always found new things to do. He loved to read and was always checking out new books from the library. He would read very awesome things. He learned something new every day. He loved Christian radio shows. He would sing and preach to people, and adults said he was a great speaker and actor. His friends and he would pretend to be Dr. Dobson and Mike Trout from Focus on the Family. He listened to Odyssey, Joy Sparton, the Sugar Creek Gang, Ranger Bill and Uncle Charly. He loved Moody Bible radio. He loved Stories of Great

13

Christians the most. He loved hearing Mile Kellogg read and Dr. Donald Cole on Open Line. Dr. Cole even came to the Allen's church once, and so did the president Dr. George Sweeting. He would love to hear Dr. Erwin Lutzer preach on Sundays. He thought he was best preacher, but loved hearing other preachers on radio as well. Of course, he loved the preachers from his churches and loved his grandpa when he preached occasionally. He was born the year his grandpa retired, so he did not hear him preach every Sunday. He was there whenever he did preach though.

His dad had found his challenge. In 6 years, he won 126 games and was 2-1 in championships. This was coming off a 7 year period when they won 11 games. All the students loved him. Some players even got some college scholarships. The school and Coach Allen was getting a good reputation around the state. The athletic program was good with his help as dean of students. His students loved his freshmen history class. And now he started looking at new challenges at other schools in the South east. He was sending out his resume to schools around the Carolinas, Georgia, and Alabama. He even sent it to a couple of colleges. Jack had wondered what it would be like to be a college coach. He wanted to help out a new program.

Joey had been the high school secretary for 3 years. She had decided to keep working at school. She had taken some local college courses, and had become a certified nurse. She helped the girls volleyball and soccer teams. She made best grades in her nursing class. She wanted to help part time at a school and help. She helped teach women's Sunday School and Bible studies and was very active in the church. Other women looked unto her as a leader and liked her a lot. She was glad to be able to do some nursing and help others, and keep an eye on her kids even more at school.

Joe's sister Lauren was on those teams. She was very active in sports. She was very pretty and popular, with many friends, male and female. In 1990, she was finishing her junior year. She had been in many school plays and was a great actress and pretty good singer. She had had a few boyfriends,

14

but was single now. She had been accepted to Ivy Bible college, and would be on their volleyball team. She would go there in fall 1991. 6 of her female high school friends were going there, and they all wanted to live on the same freshmen hall. 4 guys were going as well, and planned to lie 2 in a room side by side. Lauren wanted to work with youth. She got a full athletic scholarship. She was happy. She had skipped the 3rd grade. The principal gave both kids the chance to skip a grade, and Joe turned it down. Lauren was set to graduate from high school in 1990. She had a natural beauty about her. She was one of the guys in a lot of ways. She could play sports and do things with guys and beat them at times and was as good as boys. She babysat some and worked as a cashier at a department store. She was homecoming queen and prom queen. She had boyfriends and kept her virginity until the day she got married. She was the most popular girl in school. She was a fantastic singer and was MVP of the volleyball and basketball teams. She would shock guys at times and could be as gross as them when she wanted. But she could be very polite and have the best of manners at times. Like we had said, her parents had taught them that. She had the best beauty and charm. All the guys wanted to date her and they all respected her. She was everyone's buddy. She made the best grades and like her brother, gave encouragement and help to many students. She helped them. She did some modeling, and was in a few pageants. She entered talent shows and won some.

Her family came to all her games and cheered her on. Her dad was the biggest fan and cheered louder than anyone. He was loved by all for his awesome cheering. He won awards.

The whole family loved sports. They also watched sports games on TV together and loved the Braves and Falcons and Carolina sports. They loved the Tar Heels in college basketball. Joe liked Georgia Bulldogs in football. He really got into sports.

Joe and Lauren were very happy and did not want to move from Carters ever. They had grown to love it very much. They knew they would probably move one day though, but they did not think they would love until at least Lauren finished high school in 1 year. They told their dad over and over they wanted to stay. They were too happy. And then their dad got a job offer from Hamptons High School in Hamptons, GA.

Chapter 2
Moving to Hamptons

His dad decided to move one more time and accept this job. All of Joe's mom's family was moving to Hamptons, Ga. Joe wanted the whole family to move to Carters. He did not want to move. Joe was again was very rebellious before and after the move. He was happy his whole family was together, but did not want to move. He acted a lot like he did before the other move for about a week or so in March. Then his mom reminded him of the talk he had had with his grandpa.

His grandpa sent him a letter telling him it would be ok. He told him once he had not wanted to move away from the family. And now he would be back together living with the whole family again. He would be in junior high and make many more friends. He was older now, and keep in touch with friends by letters and phone calls. He even told him one day they could talk on computer, he had heard that may happen in a few years.

Joe wanted to please his grandpa always. He loved him so very much. He did not want to disappoint him. Or his parents. Joe was always mature for his age, and again apologized for being a rebel. He calmed down and once again acted like a good boy again. Joe worked hard to get the house ready for sale. He was always good on doing his chores, and he worked even harder now.

Joe had been cutting people's grass since he was 10. He was good at earning money and saving it. He was very good at building a bank account. He made baseball cards and sold them. He would make stuff for people, and they would pay him. He was good in art and crafts. He was getting good in electronics and fixing stuff. He was leaning a lot about computers. Papa gave the family 3 computers for Christmas. One was for the parents, and there was one apiece for Joe and Lauren. They loved playing computer games and typing papers on it for school. It made things easier. Joe could be on the computer for several hours. Joe started doing fake baseball teams and leagues and players and such on the computer. He had a lot of fun. He designed things for people on the computer. He fixed things for people. He would fix things for people and program VCRS and would do it for just a few dollars. People liked him and depended on him. He decided he would do the same thing in Hammonds. His parents got a house with an extra garage so he could have a weight room there as well. He loved to keep in shape. He would keep up same work he did in Georgia.

The family got new jobs in Hammonds. His Uncle Fred would be a professor at the Bible college. His other uncle would be the assistant catering manager at the Bible college cafeteria, and be a cashier. His aunt would be working at the local junior college. Everyone was excited about being all together again. It was strange to see his grandparent's home for sale. They had lived there for 51 years. But the whole family would be all together off same highway in the new city. His mom was excited about her new job. Some of the older cousins would work at local restaurants and stores. Hammonds was a growing community around the Bible college and junior college. More and more homes were being built and new businesses and retailers were coming. They finally got a Super Wal mart. The city was growing by bounds.

Lauren was about to graduate from high school. Her parents had waited until she graduated before moving so she would not have to start over at a new school her senior year. Now she had graduated, she was ready to move on. She would miss everyone, but was excited about living with her whole family again, this time in Georgia. She was going to leave anyways for Ivy Bible College.

She had some long talks about her friend Heather with her parents. Heather's parents were rich and only had 2 kids, she had a sister named Nena. They were going to Europe for a year to experience a different culture. They had offered to let Lauren come too. She wanted to go. She had always wanted to live there. The Vowells would live in England for the summer, Spain in the winter, Germany for 2 months, and France for 2 months. They were millionaires and would pay all her expenses. Lauren begged to go.

One night, her parents promised her a decision the next morning. They talked late until the night. The next morning, the last week of school, they came downstairs to breakfast Joe and Lauren were anxious. Joe wanted his sister to be able to go as well.

Her parents smiled. Joey said "You can go. You can live with your friend Heather see Europe. We want you to see the world. It will give you the best chances. You will have an awesome experience. We will miss you, but trust the Vowell's. You can live with them and see Europe. It will be a life changing experience, and will always be something to cherish. We want you to be able to do these things while you are still young."

Joe and Lauren squealed and ran and hugged their parents. "Thank you, thank you, thank you," she said over and over again. They were so happy. Everyone at school was happy that Lauren was able to go. They had a good last week of school.

Joe would see people until they would move in July. So he would have plenty of time left with their friends.

She graduated in late May to the highest honors. They retired her jerseys from the teams. She was honored in every way. She had gifts from all boys who liked her. She had many good friends there, and spent time with them. She loved the school and town. She would miss it in a lot of ways. She had been there for 6 years, and had finished junior high and high school there. She had been filled with love from many people. But she wanted to see Europe. And she was always one who did not like to stay in one place too long. She had always enjoyed traveling. She wanted to see the country and the world. New places and new opportunities were always exciting new challengers for her. She welcomed new places. She had done a couple of short term mission trips. She enjoyed helping others, and would do it no matter what. She would start college at Ivy Bible College in 1991. That was always the only college she ever wanted to attend. And since she would be attending almost completely free, it made it all the better. She had a bright future. She wanted to marry and have 3 kids one day. And she wanted to be as good as a parent as hers were. Her mom was her hero.

Joe went swimming a lot at the neighborhood pool and at friend's houses. One day in late June, he even skinny dipped one last time. Joe did crazy jumps. He always wore flowered polka dotted bathing suits, which amused everyone. He was a good swimmer, and could stay under for a long time, longer than most anyone. Everyone liked swimming, and they had great fun. They had some fun parties. They also played a lot of baseball and soccer games. All the friends spent time together daily. Joe spent time with each one of his friends and made them happy. He promised to stay in touch with everyone. He bought gifts for all the good friends, especially the girls. Everyone bought farewell gifts for him as well. Joe had been a good friend and everyone would miss him very much. They all loved him and respected him. Lauren and Joe had built tree houses and clubhouses in the woods. This is where their friends and they loved to play. They had some cool stuff in there, even little TVs and radios. Joe could spend hours in the woods playing. He and his friends had built the tree houses and clubhouses themselves. They were good carpenters. Joe liked to work with his hands and build things. He felt good at times. He would help his parents around the house as well.

Joe wrote a book about what Carters had meant to him. He talked about how he had even not even wanted to move there. He wrote all about his experiences and what the town meant to him. Everyone loved his book, it was only 22 pages and it got it published locally. Many people bought copies, it was only $2. People loved reading all about them and him.

The moving day came around late June. Again, all the friends in the area helped them move. They had a big celebration for them at Heather Vowell's house. It was to be rented out for a year. Joe and Lauren put on a show for all to see. They put on skits, played the piano, and Joe told his jokes and did his imitations. Joe had gotten really good doing imitations of people. Some were famous, some were people they knew. It cracked everyone up. He told a lot of jokes, some he had just heard, and some he had just made up. He sang some wacky songs he had written. He gave everyone a comic strip story he had written. Everyone loved it and was glad. It made them laugh. His drawings and animals were as crazy as always. He used to watch the Wuzzles TV show, when 2 animals were in one. It inspired him to make up some unique animals. He also wrote a special song. Some friends sang some Michael W Smith songs, and thanked them for all they had done there. They got some good gifts, and people presented them with some special photo albums of their 6 years there. There were some very special photos and memories in the books. All of Joe's friends had written beside their pictures how much Joe meant to them. They wrote special things. Joe had to get extra pages for his yearbook for people to sign, because so many people wanted to sign it and tell him how much he meant to them. Even the high schoolers signed it, and told him they would miss him. All of Lauren's female friends

21

loved him. They even took him on special outings and dances, despite him only being in 6th grade. All the high school guys invited him to play sports with him, and he was one of the 1st guys picked for the teams. He was good at sports, especially for his age. He led the teams in a lot of categories, and was also very unselfish and helped others get better. People respected him. He was the leader of the guys his age. He was feeling very fortunate to make such good friends. He hoped he could make some new good friends like these when they moved to Georgia. Their parents figured he would. He was a big time people person who encouraged everyone he met. He was a great help to all.

One night, they gathered at the school for a special program. The school honored his dad for turning around the basketball team and helping out the athletic programs. Jack's assistant would take over coaching, but knew he had some big shoes to fill. Mike Thompson was a local insurance salesman who had always enjoyed sports. He had always helped coach, and was now going to be a head coach. He had quit the insurance agency and now would work in the school development office.

Joe had a real tough time saying bye to Anna. He had been going with her for a few months. They had kissed and made out a few times. She was the first girl he slept in same bad with, but nothing happened beyond that. They were breaking up because they did not want to do the whole long distance thing. They had grown very close and liked each other a lot. But they were moving on and it was sad to say goodbye. They promised to keep in touch and hugged and kissed goodbye. She meant a lot to Joe and she would always be his 1st love and he would always remember good things of her. When they had been real little kids, he had pushed her on the swings and pretended it was a train. She was his first female friend since he moved there. She was the coolest girl he knew. He wished her only the very best.

He and his friends played some wild games. They played basketball "horse" with really long words that took a long time.

They played crazy games of flag football that took a long time. They talked of crazy wild stuff. They took crazy basketball shots. They drank a lot of sodas and ate a lot of pizzas. They had the craziest truth or dares. They were sad Joe was going though. Joe gave girls presents and they gave some to him. He made them stuff and built the stuff and gave them stuffed animals. He spent time with them and told them stories. He drew pictures of them together and gave them to them. They loved and appreciated that. He prayed with them. He shared funny jokes and stories. They would stay in touch by emails and letters and phone calls.

Joe was thankful for his awesome friends and that God had given him such awesome friends. And he remembered he did not even want to move there, and now he did not want to move. He would miss them a lot, and he spent lots of time with them. He was glad he could meet all them and stay in touch.

The family took a vacation together. They unpacked all the furniture at their new home in Hamptons around June 20th. They went through Alabama and spent some time in Florida. They went down to Disney World and had a fun good time. They had old friends who lived there and spent some good quality time there. They went to most every place in the Orlando area. They were very impressed with the space station. They learned much history. Joe thought it was a lot like the trip to Washington, DC they took in 1988. He loved seeing the buildings and history there. It was very cool.

On the 4th of July, the whole family gathered at the state park at the beach. They rented some cabins there, and some stayed at a lodge. They had a good time together. Jack's family joined them for a couple of days. Other people would watch them and smile. They had always enjoyed going to the state park for a few years. They met new friends every summer. Joe and his cousins would stay in sleeping bags in the den area. They felt it was like camping out in a way. Sometimes they did when they were spending the night at each other's houses. They thought it was always a lot of fun. Joe and 2 cousins his age built a sand castle that was real nice and big. They even won a sand castle contest. They went to a water park one day. It was a lot of fun. Joe always liked the water parks like that. They were there most of the day. He went down the longest slides the most. He did not like the long rides though. They also did some tubing. The next day they went to a little amusement park. Joe was never a big fan of roller coasters. He went on some and had some fun. He did not want to go backwards or upside down though. He rode on the more tame roller coasters. He enjoyed the shows the people put on and hugged the characters and had his pictures taken with them. They went to see a couple of minor league baseball games, and that was a lot of fun. Everybody enjoyed that a lot. He loved minor league games and meeting the players. He spent good time with them and joked with them in the bullpen and laughed. He sat right behind the visitor's bullpen. Some of them became great big leaguers. He was able to brag he had met them. He had the coolest chants and signs and they had the most fun at the games. He loved minor league games a lot.

And then the whole family gathered in Hamptons. They would all live in the same area, there was 3 neighborhoods that joined together, all with new homes. A man had owned a large farm and woods, and sold 3/4 of his land to the city to build. Joe was glad the whole family would be so close together, and was looking forward to being with them. And he was excited about what happen to them in Hamptons.

Chapter 3
The Teen Years

Once again, Joe adjusted well. He started junior high at Hamptons Middle School, where his dad taught history and coached basketball and helped in football. He did some dares, and was sweet to the ladies, and became very popular again. Despite the fact he had all the girls, no guy could hate him because of his daring, fun personality, and how cool he was in all the areas.

He played junior high basketball and baseball. He led the team in assists, and was third in points. In baseball, he led the team in hits as a hitter and strikeouts as a pitcher. He was on the school newspaper and continued his cartoons and advice column. He also wrote a sports column. He would take photos for the school yearbook. And despite all that, he continued to make good grades. In games he did not play in, he would cheer louder than anyone. He led pep rallies. He helped others in school work. He helped others in advice. He sought out the nerds, and ate and hung out with them. He enjoyed the 7th grade and was ready to become a teenager. He kept in touch with old friends, and even visited there a few times.

Lauren loved Europe. She took up a whole photo album of photos. It was an awesome experience for her. She made some awesome memorable memories. She talked for hours of all she had seen there. She saw so many historic sites. She met so many people. She took a lot of tours. She went to lots of teachers. She met some famous people and got autographs. She loved everything on the trip. She loved spending time with Heather's family. She grew to love them very much.

Joe built new clubhouses and tree houses. He helped people in electronics and carpentry. He would mow people's lawns and clean their bathrooms. He kind of liked custodial work. He had a weight room in the garage. He joined the local YMCA. He loved to swim a lot. He ran and walked a lot and stayed in good shape. He played basketball and baseball with his friends.

The whole family was there in the city. Joe's grandma died in her sleep in August 1991. And Papa died in January 1992. Joe was going to miss his grandparents a lot. He had loved them dearly, and always respected them a lot and wanted to please them.

Joe became a teenager in June 1991. He finished junior high on some good notes. He was starting to stray some from God some, but was getting better and better in sports. He was captain of the middle school squads and played JV basketball some in last games. He was the editor of the school paper, and his comics and column and photos he took around school were the most popular around school. People got the paper just for his material. He was already the most popular boy in the middle school, and was very happy at that. He graduated in May 92, and was ready for high school the next fall.

Lauren loved Bible college. She wrote him a lot, and told him to be good. She was a good player and was very popular. She dated 2 guys who did not work out. She started going out with a guy named Mark Taylor around March of her freshmen year and was very happy. She started some games, and led all

26

freshmen in volleyball stats. Her coach relied on her help a lot. He and his friends would make up TV shows and radio shows on tape. They acted like newscasters and Djs and talk show hosts. They watched ESPN and pretended to be Sports Center anchors. They watched the news for ideas. Soon, he stopped listening to Christian music and shows. He even stopped listening to his old favorite Christian radio show Adventures in Odyssey, and started listening to punk music. He loved music with profanity he would listen to.

He did start straying some. He did not want to go to youth group activities as much. He hung out with some rowdy guys and girls and smoked some and cussed some. He started dating a few girls, and lost his virginity on his 14th birthday to a girl named Cindy. He slept with around 3 girls the next year, and each time it did not work out. He did not care anymore about waiting for marriage. Hc did not want to be a good Christian boy anymore. He started drinking some. He was not a good church boy at times. His parents did know how he was acting up. They did pray for him and talk to him because they knew he smoked some and had a rowdy group of friends. They knew he was tired of church at times. They prayed every day. They prayed he would come back to God and be good again and all that.

In May 1993, he was finishing the 9th grade. He had survived the torment of the seniors, even being and thrown in girl's locker room 3 times. He played JV basketball and was a key player in the championship. He played 6 games on varsity and scored 25 points. He led the JV baseball team in doubles, and had 3 hits including a homer for the varsity.

He was very popular. He wrote for the high school newspaper. He took part in all the school dramas and musicals. He made up the craziest stuff.

But his dad took him for a long drive through the country one day. He wanted to have a long and serious talk with his son. He knew he was not acting like he should and was rebelling a lot. His sister was home, and he would not listen to her advice. She brought Mark for a visit, and Joe was not being hospitable to him. His mom had suggested Jack take Joe for a ride.

Jack told his son he was acting up too much. "Son, we know you are not acting right. Your new best friends are not Christians, and we have heard some not so good stuff about them. We have heard you smoked with them and a girl told us she heard you cussing some. Son, we love you. We want you to be the best kid you can be. You have always been very smart and mature. Older kids seek you out, and younger kids look up to you. You don't want to let people down, and you want to be a role model. I know you sometimes get tired of church and being a good Christian boy. But it is good for you. You are a good athlete. God gave you some good gifts. You are very sensitive to others and have a good heart. I want you to be better and hang out with Christian guys and don't mess around with girls. I know you like dancing and kissing, but don't let it get too far. We pray for you, and we love you. We don't want you to get into trouble."

Joe thought how little they knew, he had already had sex with some girls. "Ok dad, I am sorry. I know I can get wild sometimes. I know the guys are not the best. I do not want to upset or disappoint you. I will try to be a good guy and follow Jesus and be a good friend. I like sports; it can be my escape at times. I will go to youth group more. I will be nicer to Lauren and Mark. I promise, Dad."

Jack smiled. "Ok son, that is all we ask. We love you son, and want the very best for you. We want you to get an athletic scholarship or writing or something. God has blessed you with so many good gifts. Use them, son. Use them as your advantage. Drama goes good to you. You can be a good preacher and speaker one day. You can teach drama. I want to see you succeed and go to college. I want you to be the biggest success story, and you can be famous, and help millions. I love you, son. We love you more than you can ever possibly know. You mean everything to us. We are proud of you. "

Joe said "I know you do, dad. I love you and Mom and Lauren very much as well too. I want to make you happy. I will be nice to them."

He and Lauren and Mark were very close the rest of Lauren's trip. People thought her and Mark would be married one day. They had dated over a year. They went to eat and drink and drank sodas together. He and Lauren had the contests they used to always have growing up. Mark joined in some. They looked at photo albums and told Mark funny stories about their past. Mark and Lauren had played with her dolls, and turned around and played with his army men. They sang and did piano and did skits and plays. Mark met a lot of the church people they liked. And they had a good visit. They pigged out on pizza and ice cream. They danced to rap music. They went to see movies at the theater together, and rented movies to watch. They walked around the neighborhoods, and visited with all the families. Sadly, on June 13, Lauren and Mark went back to Ivy to take summer school 2 sessions. Joe was sorry to see them go.

He started working Sundays as a bus boy at the Banana House in August. The restaurant was very crowded and many workers were needed on Sundays. He washed dishes some. They were open 11-3, and finished around 4:30. He enjoyed working at the restaurant very much. He was a good worker and worked very hard. He kept the workers entertained and the workers and customers all loved him. The boss gave him a raise after just a couple of months, as more people from his church were coming in and eating there, on Sundays, and doing the week. Business went up.

Joe went to Atlanta one weekend and had a lot of fun at Six Flags. He saw the Braves, went to White Water, and Stone Mountain. He had a great time.

When school started in fall 1993, he was hanging around bad crowd again. He was smoking and drinking and could cuss with the best of them. And then something wonderful happened. Susan Overton moved to town. She had lived in Hamptons until she was 6. A lot of the kids remembered and loved her. She lived in Carters for 6 months, and was in Joe's 4th grade class that fall. She too could be wild. Her parents were into drugs and alcohol. She learned how to cuss from them. She had a reputation for sleeping around with guys in middle and high school. She even slept with some girls as she explored life. Joe and her started dating in September 1993, and slept together many times. Joe was lying to his parents, pretending to be hanging out with some church boys, who would cover for him. He started acting very wild. He played JV basketball. Now he was in 10th grade, there was talk of bringing him to varsity. He wanted to win another championship.

In December, Joe and Sally got drunk at a party and went upstairs to a bedroom. They woke up to cops in the house. Everyone was in big trouble. Joe was yelled at. His parents cried. They wanted him to reform. They found out he had been lying to them. People told them Joe has been drinking and smoking and even tried pot. He had a reputation for sleeping with many girls. His parents grounded him for 3 months, and forbid him to see Sally. But she was still his girlfriend, and he got to call her and talk to her at school some. He could not hang out with his friends as much, but half the school was grounded anyways. He was allowed to keep playing basketball, but 3 games were forfeited due to suspensions. The students also got a 2 week suspension from school. The punishments were strict and severe.

Joe's parents had the pastor, youth director, and the president of a nearby Christian college talk to him. They prayed for him. They took the TV and computer out of his room. They did give him some freedoms, and did not want to lose him forever. They told him daily they loved him very much.

On February 1st, Sally came up to him in science class and told him they needed to talk at lunch about something serious. Before, they had always eaten together near a willow tree near the cafeteria. It was their spot. Joe met her there at 12:20 for lunch. Here is some of the talk, with the profanity cut out.

Sally went 1st. "Joe, I have some bad news for you. I do not know how to tell you this. I know you remember the big party and how we had sex again?"

Joe said "Yea, no one could ever forget hat party as long as we live, no matter how much some people want to forget it. Bad times."

Sally sighed. "Joe, I, Um. Joe.."

Joe said softly "Go ahead, honey, say it. What's wrong?"

Sally cried a little. "I'm pregnant, Joe. I am pregnant. We were too drunk that night to do protection. I am so sorry, Joe, so sorry."

Joe got upset for a minute, then saw Sally sobbing. He held her close, and let her cry on his shoulder, He held her there and tried to comfort her. "It's ok, baby, it will be ok, I promise you. Everything will work out, and everything will be ok, and you will be all right. I will be here for you always. You can always count on me. I will be the best I can be. It will be ok."

Sally cried. "No, no, no, and it's my fault. I slept around. I had sex with so many guys. I asked for this. You sleep with girls. Sometimes I feel like a terrible person. I hate myself sometimes. We are just 15, we are too young to be parents. We don't know a dang thing."

Joe talked to her. He told her good things. He told her everyone has sex with people, and experiment. He told her he loved her. They sat around and discussed what to do. They discussed abortion, adoption, keeping the baby, what all to do. They talked about how to tell the parents. His parents would be so upset. Her parents would cuss her out as always and pretty soon would not even care or notice. They were drunk more and more all the time now, and got high a lot. They talked after school about all the best options and what they should do. They finally decided to tell the parents that Friday night the 5th.

It came in a hurry. Joe and Sally sat his parents down and told them around 8:00. His parents were devastated. They both cried a lot. Joe cried some too. He kept telling his parents he was so sorry over and over again. Sally said she was very sorry as well. They said Sally's cousin, who lived a few homes down, and was not into drugs or drinking, had decided to keep care of her baby. She was 22, and because of an accident,

31

could not have kids. She was married to a man named Timmy. So Sally would have the baby in September, and give it to her cousin. They all knew Sally and Joe were too young to have a kid. Sally's home was not a good one, (even Sally admitted that.). And the Allens could not keep a kid anymore.

After Sally left after 9, his parents talked for 15 minutes to be by themselves for a few moments to cool down some and think of new ways to help him. They knew they had slept around before marriage, and even conceived Lauren before they were married. In a lot of ways, they were in no position to judge. But he was their teenage son who had messed up. They came over and sat down and talked to Joe by himself for a little bit. They needed to talk to him about some stuff.

"Mom, Dad, I know I have been messing up. I know I have greatly saddened and disappointed you before, especially now with this news. I am so sorry. I cannot tell you how sorry I am. I am so sorry, I hope you are not too saddened by this. Please forgive me." He started crying a little. "I do not know why I keep messing up. Please help me change."

His parents were crying. They did not know what to say. They told him they were sad and disappointed. But they would always love him no matter what. He was their son, and they knew he was trying. They wanted him to succeed. And they told him it would be ok.

Jack said "Son, we all mess up. No one is perfect. We got pregnant with Lauren out of wedlock. We both had sex as teenagers. Joe, son, we all goof up. We see the consequences of our mistakes. Some are bigger than others, like this. We will stand behind you and support ya'll and love ya'll. God will never abandon you or leave you. We will always be your parents and love you."

Lauren cried over the phone when he told her. She told him a lot of the things his parents had told him. She told him she loved him and it would be all right.

Basketball was all right the rest of the season. The whole family and school and church learned of pregnancy. He was shunned by some of the Christian kids, and some tried to help them even more. In February, Joe led the JV team to a championship. He played for the varsity a little at the end of the season. They won the championship as well, and Joe felt on top of the world.

In April, Sally found out she was having twins. She was happy she would have 2 babies. Joe was kind of happy as well. Her cousin was happy she could have 2 kids to take care of now. She had been sad when she could not have kids, she loved kids. She was ready for September.

Joe had been doing good and going to church. He had been trying to live good again. He was doing good on Bible memory work. He was helping people by giving advice. The varsity baseball team improved by 12 games and made the state semifinals. He acted like a Christian again, and hung out with some good guys, and they helped him out. He was acting like his old self.

It did not last. He started hanging out with the bad crowd again. On June 1st, Joe celebrated his 16th birthday by getting his driver's license. He and his friends drove some. Late that night, he sneaked out of the house. They smoked some pot and drank some beer. They climbed on a hill of rocks and acted crazy. Joe was running and slipped down the hill. His left leg was broken. He missed work for 2 months, and was in the hospital for almost a week. He was mad at God. He thought God may be after him to finally truly become a Christian. He almost turned to God. He thought he may be getting punished for all the misdeeds he had done. Then, he rebelled even more. He turned his back on God. He quit athletics and moved in with Sally. His parents were very saddened. He was only 16. Lauren tried to talk sense into him, but he cussed her out and threw things at her, and she ran out crying. His parents tried to make him move back home, he was underage. He had kept running away no matter how tough they made it. They finally just said enough was enough. He was being mean to cousins, family, smoking pot, drinking beer, cussing non stop. He no longer went to church. His funny stories and jokes and advice had long quit. He quit writing for school paper and stopped giving advice and helping others. He refused to talk to Christians. He would cuss at them. He listened to profanity laced music, and had the worst friends. He became a drug dealer, and became rich and dressed snazzy. He continued to work on Sundays at the restaurant.

On September 4, 1994, the 16 year old couple had 2 babies. The twins were identical girls, Michelle and Rebecca. They were very excited. Lauren's cousin Lisa got them after 3 days. Timmy and Lisa had 2 little girls to care of, and were so close to Sally and Joe's home. Sally's mom was killed in a drug overdose that weekend, and they could have cared less. Sally's dad was away so much they hardly ever saw him. Joe quit school that December when the semester was over. At Christmas time, Lauren came by and told them her and Mark were getting married in May 1995. It would be after graduation, because the whole family would be there. She wanted Joe there. He promised to be there. He was very sweet during the whole day, and apologized for being such a jerk that one day back. She forgave him, and they hugged. They had one big contest for the fun of it, and played some cards. They spent time with the family for Christmas. Joe behaved well the whole team and was a good guy. Everyone was happy to see him. Sally brought the babies by. Everybody loves babies, and held them and loved them. It was a very good time for all, and a great Christmas and New Years.

Joe went to work full time at the restaurant in September 1994. He was working 40 hours a week. He loved the Banana House. His injuries had completely healed. He was washing dishes and working harder than anyone. Everyone there liked him very much. He was a very popular worker. He quit dealing drugs and dropped the druggies from his friends. He felt better.

Joe spent that spring in the usual stuff. Sally and he lived together in her home. They got drunk 2 days a week. She went to work at Wal Mart and part time at Banana House as the hostess/ cashier. They traveled with his family to Lauren and Mark's graduation and wedding in May 1995. They went to Ivy and Lansing and showed Sally and the younger kids where they used to live. They had a good weekend and few days in South Carolina. He showed her the church his grandpa had pastored for 37 years, and the home for 50 years.

Sally was fascinated to learn about the history and more about the families. She loved the love they showed. She had grown up in a terrible home situation and envied his family. She decided she wanted to spend more time with them at home back in Hamptons. Sally's heart was starting to change. She wanted to know more about God and more of church and Jesus. She saw how important God was to the family, and was interested. She asked a lot of questions, and learned a lot. But they loved partying too much. Sally and Joe attended church some and read Bible some, but it was nothing serious.

That fall, they got their GEDS. They were quitting drugs and drinking and cussing less. They only used the mild cuss words now. They were reading Bibles more and attending church more. They started sleeping in separate bedrooms, and went no further than making out. They started praying together. It appeared his parents and family's prayers were working.

On September 1, Joe was taking a nap. He jumped out of bed with a shout. It was 3:22 PM. He was home alone and a strange sensation came over him. He had a dream a baby was born and went to him. Then an angel pointed at him. He did not know what to think. Little did he know, that moment in Oakley, Virginia a little girl was being born to a local Bible college dean of men. Michelle Marks, who would one day be his wife, and true love, had just been born. But Joe did not know what had happened. He just thought he had a strange dream, and got over it in a few minutes. He just did not understand that strange sensation. One day, in many years, he would find out.

Starting in 1996, Joe worked full time at a computer store fixing computers at Moonie Computers. He would still work at Banana House, but it was closed on Saturdays now to give people a day off, especially the owners. Plus he was awesome on computers, and people would ask for him. He still spent quality time with Sally. She was working full time at Banana House as a cashier/hostess. She loved the job very much and they enjoyed working together very much. They were a popular couple in the area, and hung out with many more couples.

Joe and Sally continued to live Ok. They eventually moved to an apartment complex, and lived on different floors. Joe was working hard. They still drank and got wild at times, but were doing all right. They had a few birthdays.

Christmas 1997 came. They spent time with his family again. Lauren was pregnant with her first kid. And things with them were going good. Occasionally, they had a relapse and got drunk and did some drugs. Sally got pregnant in June 1997, and miscarried in late July. Joe and Sally refused to go to church anymore. They were mad at God. They decided if God was punishing them. They could punish God. They started acting up again, and rebelling. They were drinking more and more. Drug tests were common, and they wanted to keep their jobs. They did not want to be in trouble with the law; they had always avoided trouble with the law before. They did not want to deal with drugs.

Joe had been up and down for a long time, many years now. He would never completely turn away from God. He also would never come to Him. He believed in God, and went to church some. But he and Sally decided they were young and liked to party too much. They loved the wild party scene and crowd. They thought Christianity had too many strict rules. They never completely turned over their lives to God. They enjoyed the fun and sin too much.

Lisa and Timmy were good foster parents to Michelle and Rebecca. In September 1997, they adopted a brother and sister. Jackson was 11 and Susan was 8. Michelle and Rebecca were 3 and were good kids. Joe and Sally were able to visit them a lot, and they stayed at their apartments some. Joe and Sally loved their kids very much and spoiled them rotten. Timmy and Lisa wanted to adopt the twins, but were never able to. Sally kept on putting it of, and saying maybe, someday.

36

Joe loved the internet. He looked at some pages he should not look at. He felt guilty sometimes. Sometimes he felt guilty. Sally too liked looking at bad pages on the internet. She felt bad, and finally stopped. They were both in love with email and emailed all the people they had known in the past and did not see anymore. They got scanners and made picture pages and their own webpages. They loved how the internet could do things instantly. They had great fun online.

Life was good. They spent much time with the families at Christmas. Sally mentioned marriage. They attended church some again. They liked the apartment building. They had dated over 4 years. They were enjoying life, and things were going pretty good.

Chapter 4
Marriage and Divorce

Joe and Sally continued to live Ok. They moved to an apartment complex in Summer 1997. They lived on different floors. Joe was working hard. They still drank and got wild at times, but were doing all right. In January 1998, they were both 19. He got down on one knee on January 13 at a romantic spot at the lake and proposed marriage. She said yes. The next few months were full of wedding preparations.

Lauren and Mark had a baby Naomi born June 13th. He was the Youth and Christian Education Director at a local church. Lauren had been his secretary, but quit due to the baby being born. She wanted to raise the baby herself. It was happy times for them. They loved Oakley very much.

Sally and Joe prepared a good wedding and invited a lot of people. There would be around 180 people at the wedding. She picked out a beautiful gown. She invited 7 friends to be bridesmaids. Lisa would be the matron of honor. Joe also had 7 men as his groomsmen. Mark was going to be the best man. Joe looked up to his brother in law and loved him dearly as he did his sister. The plans went good and they planned to marry at the Hamptons Baptist church. Joe had invited old friends from his old towns as a boy. Sally had lived there for years. Everyone was excited and planned to come. Joe spent his last day at the Banana House that Saturday before the wedding after 5 years, but everyone there was coming. He was well loved at the restaurant. People from Granton's would be there. It was closed for the day, except to cater the wedding.

The week of the wedding went by good. Sally's family was not so far away either. Her dad gave her away. The rehearsal dinner went smoothly. The wedding and reception went very good. Joe and Sally were married September 19, 1998. They were both 20. They honeymooned in the Bahamas for a week and then moved back into Sally's old home they had shared together. Her dad left her $300,000 after he had become rich in a lottery. They were living very comfortably then. Sally gave him $ 130,000 to keep, no matter what ever happened to them. They could have stopped working for a while, but they both loved working and not being bored. Joe took a 2nd job at a movie theater in November. He quit the restaurant in February 1999. Sally became a secretary at Hamptons Middle School in January, and only worked 2 nights at the restaurant.

At Christmas, they took in the kids. They were 20 and could take care of 3 year old girls. Lisa and her husband had the 2 kids, and a 3 year old Chinese girl coming in January. They always knew Sally would want her kids when she got older and could properly take care of them.

Marriage was good. It was off to a rough start at times. But they had lived together before and dated so many years. They acted like a married couple in many ways before. They truly loved each other and were very happy being married. Life was going very good. They attended church every other Sunday, and drank every once in a while. They spent time with the families and were growing closer and closer all the time to the families.

39

The twins loved living with their families. They loved to visit Lisa a lot, especially after Sue arrived. They loved the little girl, who was just a couple of months younger than they were. They played all kinds of fun games and enjoyed life. They were very obedient.

Joe started taking college courses at the local junior college. He took courses from Fall 1999-Spring 2000 and got a certificate in Computer technician. Starting in 2000, he loved working at the movie theater on the weekends. He worked as an usher and some as a cashier. He liked being an usher the very best. He did get tired of all the customer's complaints and stupid questions/ remarks. He had never known so many stupid people as those customers. They would ask where the bathroom was, when it was right there. People would go into movies before the ushers had a chance to clean movies. They would even sit down before the other movie was over and ruin the end of the movie for themselves. When they sat down before the ushers cleaned it, and then complain the movie was dirty. Joe could not understand why they would do that. Usually, he would say if they wanted to sit in a dirty theater, they could do just that. Joe found all kinds of stuff people had left behind, like money and purses and cans and wallets and pacifiers and bottles and books and cell phones. He ended up working there for 7 years until 2005. In 1999, he was a shift leader. He loved working in the box office in slow periods. He was great in customer service and was polite and nice to everyone. Again, he was very popular. All the high school kids loved his stories and jokes. He would write comic strips and stories and draw pictures for people. He would help everyone with schoolwork and people started making better grades. He would help with relationship advice, and enjoyed hanging out with the guys after work at times.

Y2k came in 2000. Lauren had a baby boy, Mark Jr in February. He became a pastor in Samson, Maryland in late 1999. They were happy and serving the Lord. Joey had retired and Jack was still at the high school. He was only an assistant basketball coach and taught 4 history courses. The students loved him very much. Most of the family has moved away from the area, but were still in Georgia, Alabama, Florida, Tennessee, or North Carolina. They still stayed close together and remained close in relationships.

Joe got a basic one year certificate this time from the junior college in Summer 2000. He took a lot of the basic courses. He was doing good. The theater had given him 2 raises. The twins had a big party that fall for their 6th birthday. People came and dressed up like Winnie the Pooh and friends. All of the kids loved that. Sally became head Administrative Assistant at the middle school. They were both making good money. They ran a part time online business and saved most of the lottery money her dad had given her. He died that summer, and everyone attended the funeral. In late 2001, they would get an additional $ 250,000 from his will.

In early 2001, Joe started drinking more and more. Sally was living a clean life and was thinking of finally becoming a Christian. Joe was drinking late at night and spending less and less time at home. His kids missed him very much and begged him to play with them more. Joe was abusive at times, and said some cruel things. He was sick of his life here and wanted some changes. He did not sleep with his wife a lot, and was not romantic at all. They hardly ever had sex. They began to fight a lot more. They would cuss each other out at times. Joe never went to church anymore. Sally was crying a lot. She kept on telling him he needed to be a better role model for the kids. She wanted to move to a new city and start over. She had lived in Hamptons for years. Everyone knew her life story, and how messed up she had been. Joe refused to think about moving. He always said no to more kids. His first home seemed to be at bars, and he loved them. He spent far more time at work at the theater then he did at home. Sally was feeling lonely, and considered an affair, but changed her mind. Counseling did not help that much. He refused to see Christian counselors or pastors. Soon, he stopped going to counseling all together.

Then, in fall 2001, he was loving again. He was great to his now 7 year old twins and was great to his wife. He came home earlier. He was bringing her presents. She thought he was being great now. He was the perfect husband again. And then came Halloween.

It was a good party at the church. The kids had a good time. He said he had some errands to run. She dropped off the kids to spend the night at Lisa's. She drove to a hotel 1 hour away to reserve a room for a romantic getaway in November. She saw Joe from a distance in the park. She was wondering what he was doing. She got closer and he was kissing a woman. She was speechless. She did not know what to do. She followed them at a distance and saw them go to the hotel room together and stayed in there. She knew they were having sex and did not know what to do. She decided to ask some questions. They had been coming there for 6 months, said a bellboy. They came 3-4 times a month. He thought they were married, since they both wore rings. He just minded his own business and never talked to them. Sally was devastated and did not what to do.

She knocked on the door the next morning and had a hotel guard with her. She caught her husband and a woman together. It was Lucy Smith, who had been 3 years behind them in school. Joe had to confess to an affair. Sally told him the marriage was over. She moved out and took most of the money. She just left Joe with the $ 130,000 she had promised him no matter what. She took the twins and moved to Herring, Tennessee. The divorce was filed and they were separated.

Joe called her some. He begged her to come home. She changed cell phone numbers and got an unlisted home number. She got an order so he could not call or bother her anymore. They saw each other in court a few times. Joe was devastated he had ruined their marriage. He wanted her back. His parents called him to their home and voiced their displeasure at him. They lectured him once again.

Jack spoke gently but firmly. "Son, you need to think about these things more. This is not a game. You broke your wife's heart. And now you need to leave her alone. You had a great wife, she was thinking of becoming a Christian, you have 2 great little girls. I don't know why you are throwing this all away. I don't know this Lucy woman, she looks pretty, but is she worth it? Is she so pretty that you need to throw away a relationship that old? Ya'll have truly gone through the best and the worst of times. She was tempted to have an affair with so many men. She told me how many men flirted with her and asked her out, but she chose to remain loyal to you. And you repay her by having an affair. You broke her heart. Ya'll can never be friends again, and it is all your fault. You have no one to blame but yourself. You need to think son, we love you always, but we want you to finally straighten out your life."

Joe felt bad, but it was too late. The divorce was final in summer 2002. He continued to date Lucy and she moved in that March. When the divorce was final, he had moved on by then.

Chapter 5
Remarriage

Joe and Lucy got together when she stared working at the theater in early 2001. She was there for 3 months, before going to a deli. She was almost 3 years younger than him. She had also been homecoming and prom queen just like Lauren. She was very pretty. She was big into music back in high school and had released a CD. She was a freshman and had a crush on the cute popular senior, but she knew she had no chance. He was dating a girl for several years and they already had 2 kids together.

Lucy Smith was born on February 2, 1982 in Fork, Florida. Her parents were good people who only drank occasionally. They were not religious, and only attended church occasionally. Her dad worked in insurance and her mom in real estate. Her brother Ted was born in April 1979 but died in 1994 in an accident.

When she was 6, they moved to Mitylene, MS. They were

there for 3 years. They then moved to Morris, Texas for 5 years. She started her freshmen year in Hammonds and knew of Joe and Sally. They moved to Lansing, South Carolina and ironically lived in Joe's old home. She moved back to Hammonds before her senior year with her family and finished high school there. She was a popular student and played soccer and softball. She was a big fan of the Atlanta Braves and had enjoyed the success of the pennants. She didn't sleep with a boyfriend until she was 18. She was 19 when she met Joe for real at a bar. They were both big Braves fans, and met watching a UNC game. They talked about the Braves chances for 2001 and went back to her place. He was only the 3rd guy she had slept with. They enjoyed the affair at the hotel. She was glad to destroy a marriage. She loved Joe, and despised Sally. She knew all about her past and called her the worst names. She loved calling Sally a skanky slut. She was glad when the separation was on, and Joe and her moved in together. She never went to church, and told Joe not to go, so they never did go. They went to Braves home games 3 times a month, and enjoyed it. They watched all the games on TV, or taped and watched later. Joe and Lucy loved the movies. They would rent 3 movies a week. They went to the movie theater and saw the new movie every single Saturday. It was nice since Joe worked there. A new crew of employees was there. They all grew to love Joe and Lucy. He still liked to drink with the guys some after work on the weekends. Lucy and Joe would take a ride through the country every Sunday afternoon. They would always enjoy it. Her family moved around a hour away in South Carolina, but they visited a lot. They saw his parents every week, and ate lunch there at least one Sunday a month. Lucy had always been very big on family stuff, and grew to love the Allens and was glad she had joined the family.

Lucy worked at a local department store for 4 years. She was a sales associate and cashier. She was very poplar and won employee of the month on a few occasions. She was given a few raises and promotions. She loved the job very much. She was finally made head cashier in 2003, which is what she had always wanted.

He heard from his mom in August 2002 that Sally had become a Christian and was attending a large Methodist church in Tennessee. She was dating the Assistant Youth director who was very popular with the kids. He was 33 and had been there 13 years. He was so popular he turned down all job offers over the years to stay there. He also coached junior high basketball and taught Middle school Bible at the local Christian school. The church knew all about Sally's life and accepted and loved her. She spoke to groups, churches, and schools sharing her new testimony. She was on fire for the Lord. She was even looking at short term mission's trip, and helping with the youth department in ways.

Joe was happy for his ex wife. He was happy she had straightened out her life and wanted to do the same. But he loved Lucy. They dated for a long time. The family liked her, even though they did not like the living together. Lauren and Mark moved to town. Mark became the pastor at the family's church. Lucy and Lauren announced their pregnancies in the summer of 2003. Over Christmas break, Joe proposed marriage to Lucy and she accepted. They planned a Sunday June 13th wedding. Lucy always wanted to get married on a Sunday, even if she really never did believe in God. Otherwise, she was a great nice person who never put down the family for their faith, and respected them, and they accepted her.

January 13, 2004 was a great day for the families. That morning, Suzanne was born to Lauren and Mark. They had wanted 3 kids, and 3 kids are what they got. And at 5:33 that afternoon, in the same room and 3 weeks early, Luke was born to Joe and Lucy and now she could be happy. She was jealous Sally had had Joe's kids, and she bore him a son. She was very contented.

Joe and Lucy were married June 13, 2004. It was a simple affair, of family, co workers, and friends. There were 60 people there, and was at the church. Mark performed the ceremony. There was 3 bridesmaids and 3 groomsmen there. It was a nice wedding and reception. Luke was there with her cousin, who was super great with kids. Sally's cousin Lisa sat in the back.

Sally did do some missionary work. She was in Spain from December 2004-March 2005. She went to area churches and spoke before she went and raised support. She was married to the Assistant youth director, who had become assistant pastor and Christian Education director. They took some time off to work in missions. They took 2 months off. They learned a lot there. Joe befriended a guy there. They showed him love and compassion and he acted like he wanted to be a Christian and asked if they would come to a meeting of his friends. Sadly, they were all atheists and they killed Sally and her husband. The youth and church were saddened. Many people came to the funeral. The youth wing was named after them. The preacher said they were martyrs for the cause of Christ. People were saved and some rededicated their lives. They had impacted many lives for Jesus. Even in death, they led people to Christ.

Michelle and Rebecca came home again. Joe was very saddened when he learned, as was his family. The girls came to their home for 2 weeks. Lucy did not want Sally's kids there. She was however sad she had died. Lisa volunteered to take in the girls again. They were 11 and in the 6th grade. Joe let them adopt them, and gave them $ 65,000 to help out. The couple who could not have kids of their own now had adopted 5 kids, 3 girls of the same age. And they felt blessed by God. They thanked Him daily.

Joe and Lucy remained married. They fought a lot at times, and got really mad at times. There was times they would cuss each other out. Joe even went to church every once in a while out of spite. But they could get very romantic and very much in love at times as well.

In October 2005, they moved to Monk, Georgia. It was in central east Georgia right near the state line. Joe had lived in Hamptons for 15 years and they wanted a break. They wanted a change in their marriage, to start over somewhere fresh. It was a small community near Augusta, which was best known for the Masters Golf tournament every Spring. They bought a home near an exclusive neighborhood off Columbia Highway. They lived in a place called Englewood, which had modest homes and was a circle of sorts. They had some very nice neighbors and made some real good friends very quickly. They fit in well. Joe and 2 of his good friends moved there and were founders and vice presidents of a computer store. They would sell computers and fix them for people. Joe also a room out back to repair stuff like TVs, DVD players, stereos, and all kinds of electronic devices. Joe still liked working on thing and repairing them. He even taught some computer classes and showed others how to be better on computers and have better skills. He built things, for he had always found very much satisfaction with putting things together.

Joe no longer worked at a movie theater, but he and Lucy still loved to see movies every weekend and rent some movies on DVD. They watched movies a lot. In January 2006, Luke had his 2nd birthday party. He was very active for a 2 year old. Joe enjoyed going to the high school basketball and baseball games again. Lucy would go, and push Luke on the swing set right near the field. Luke loved to swing and play with his stuffed animals on the swing. He played with them non stop at home. He was easily entertained by silly shows and silly toys. He was a good little boy, and was well loved by everyone who thought he was so cute and adorable. All the girls wanted to baby-sit him. Joe was already teaching him how to play sports some, with a little hoop, little bat and ball, little football. He even had a little golf club and ball. Luke would line up little bowling pins in hallway and roll ball and always go "Fall!" and "Strike !" no matter how many pins would fall. Bowling in the hall was his favorite game of all. And he sure did love when his daddy played with him.

2006 was a good year. In July, he started a Sunday comic strip. It was in 7 papers in Georgia. He had started doing this in March. He was becoming a little famous. They were making some good money from the strip. There were requests from more newspapers.

2007 and 208 were ok years. Lucy and Joe had a typical

marriage. They did fight a lot, and always made up. Joe saw his girls times a year, and loved time with them. She got a job at Lowe's and loved it. She got several raises and promotions. She was a head cashier and shift leader. Luke was 4. The comic strip was in 50 newspapers.

Joe was always bringing up gifts and toys and jewelry for her. He and Lucy still drank a lot, and hardly ever went to church. They fought a lot, but it never got abusive. And they always made up. It seemed like their marriage could survive the bad times and be like most any other marriage. They loved the town and the people. They even went to 2 Masters days. Luke was in k-4 and turned 5 in January 2009. Things were going good for the young Allen family.

And then came 2010.

Part Two:
Getting Saved
and
Bible College

Chapter 6
Getting Saved

Joe was never really truly happy. Sure he felt he had before had a great wife at times who he could love very much despite the fights at times, and he had a wonderful job. He had a kid at home and 2 at another house he saw most Saturdays and played with them some. He had 2 great jobs, was rich, and a little famous from a Sunday comic strip and a book. He loved his job on computers and fixing them, and loved customers, and was loved back. Everything seemed great on surface. Only a couple of counselors and close friends knew he and Lucy were now having marital problems. Nothing ever made him happy. He tried religion as a kid. His parents had made him to go to church. He memorized Bible, acted like a Christian, said the right things, and was a leader. But he was never truly saved. He was showing off to others. He was doing things because he had to. And he had gotten far away from it. He tried other religions. Nothing made him happy, not even money, sex, power, women, fancy homes and clothes and cars, great relationships, alcohol, drugs, children. He always felt a serious void in his life. He tried to fill it in many ways. Athletics did it for a while, but he gave up on it, and lost a lot of his step. He was not that good anymore. He explored Mormons, Buddhists, Muslims, Jewish faiths, and tried all kinds of things. He even tried being an atheist like Lucy, but always believed there was a God. He did not know where to turn. He dabbled in the occult, and hated it. He was lost.

On October 1, 2009 he was in serious depression. Lucy and he had been drifting apart. She slept at the neighbor's some nights. He would sleep in their son's room or the couch. She wanted nothing to do with God, and he was willing to try Him out again. She cussed him out for going to church. He made her happy. He was living for her, and it was an act. He did not love her anymore. He was sick of this game. He wanted out somehow and to start other anew. He was willing to try anything.

He told her he wanted to go to church, and did not care what she thought. He told her he needed faith in a God now and wanted to know more of Him. She cussed him out very much, using the words 15 times each. She packed up her stuff and said she was sick of him and his sorry attitude and she was going to her cousin's house and taking Luke with her. She needed to protect him from Joe. He needed to get his head back on his shoulders and realize what was right and what was wrong. She was sick of his act and her act. He needed to straighten out or he would lose her forever, and she did not care anymore. She was gone that night, and so was Luke. Joe was living all by himself, and in a way was relieved.

Joe started going to various churches. He had met a lovely young woman at work named Megan Moore who had a married sister named Lindsay Falls. Megan was a strong Christian and worked with finances for the computer store. She was a Christian, and people knew it. But she did not shove Jesus down anyone's throats like some people he knew. He was sick of Christians who always preached at people and told them to accept Jesus because the end was near. He respected Megan and Lindsay for their faith. Lindsay's husband Tommy was a good Christian and a big sports fan. Megan reminded him of his sister Lauren, except she was well mannered all the time. She was ok pretty, but not beautiful and she was not the type of girl to out gross the guys. Lindsay was 24 and Megan 22 and just out of college. She sang all right, but nothing special. She loved the Braves, and the Georgia Bulldogs, as did Joe. She loved the same games that he and Lauren had played growing up. She made average grades in school. She was born June 7, 1987 and had always lived in Georgia. She dated a few guys, but none worked out. She was buddies with Joe, but he was still married, and she did not date Christians, and would be a virgin when she married. Joe came on to her one night, and was surprised and pleased she took a stance. He was very sorry and promised her it would never happen again. He respected her. She told him she would pray for him and hoped he would come to Jesus one day and see He loved him very much. She told him she would pray things with Lucy worked out, but if he became a Christian, and she was an atheist, they would have to get a divorce because God did not like Christians and non Christians together. Well, the divorce is what she believed. She was a good, fun, nice person, and the sweetest person around.

Joe did not know what to think at times. He was not with a wife and kid now. He lived alone. His neighbors brought him a lot of food that was easy to make. He bought a lot of canned food and frozen food that just required putting in the microwave. He fell in love with frozen pizzas. He sought solace with beer at times. Sometimes he got drunk. He always felt real guilty at times. He knew drinking would never really solve his problems and would not really help him at all. At times, it seemed to make things even worse.

Joe tried meth twice, and hated it with a passion. He tried material things and it failed too. He started hanging out with some wild friends for a couple of months, but quit that when he cut back on his drinking to a few beers at home and only Saturday night at the bars. He worked even harder at his job. He became a workaholic at times. He needed a break, and for 2 weeks went places. He went to Disney World and Orlando and

Tampa places. He was like a kid again at Disney. He went to Six Flags in Atlanta and attended 7 Braves home games and they went 6-1. He met some players. He was feeling great. His coworkers had made him go and he was glad. They were glad he had a good vacation, and was feeling better. They hired a new Assistant manager to take some stress off of him and they helped out more. He also had a young man in college helping him fix things in the back shop. It was becoming very poplar, and he enjoyed the help. He got along with Brian, and they talked about a lot of stuff. Brian was a Mormon, and invited him to his church. Joe even went a few times, and read the Book of Mormon, but never really got into it that much. He was not sure of it all.

Joe did get depressed at times. He missed having a wife with him in bed. Joe at times thought God could never save him. He felt he had sinned too much and was too far gone. He needed some good males to talk to. He needed good mature Christians to talk to. He was even attending the church a lot where his family went. That is where Mark preached. He attended Lindsay and Megan's church some too. He talked to Christian leaders at churches and Christian counselors. There was someone besides Mark he trusted a lot now. He had a few heart to heart talks with Lindsay's husband, Tommy. He told him he had sex with many women. He told him of the rebellion, the cussing, drinking, and drinking. He told him of all the stuff he had done and gone through. He told him of the emptiness he felt in his life. He bared his soul for him, and all that was eating him up on the inside, and about what he was feeling. He did not hold anything back.

Tommy listened to all this quietly. He pondered it. He prayed in his head. He prayed out loud for Joe. He wanted to say all the right stuff. He was glad Joe was exploring the truth and wanted to know more of God and what was out there for him there.

He talked to him gently. "Joe, God will love you always. He has agape love, unconditional love. He will always be there for you, forever and ever. He wants you to come to Him. The

56

Bible says if there was 100 sheep, and only 1 was lost, the owner would look for it and rejoice when he found it. God was looking for us. He wanted us to come to Him. King Manasseh in the Bible was a wicked king. He was Hezekiah's son and was a terrible man. He had much idol worship. He was very evil and killed many people. God humbled him when he was put in prison, and he repented. He is in Heaven. Saul killed many Christians, and God saved him, and he became Paul, one of the leaders of the early church. Ted Bundy killed many women, and he became a Christian. No one is too far gone. God will save anyone who turns to him. But you have to repent and make Jesus Lord of your life and accept Him as Lord of your life. You need to make Him King of your life, and believe in Him always. Jesus is the only way to Heaven, the only way to everlasting life in Him."

Tommy shared the Bible with him. Joe had learned the verses, but never truly was with them and knew them. He showed him John 3:16, Romans 3:23 and 6:23. He showed him John 14, where Jesus went to prepare rooms in Heaven for believers. This is where Jesus says He is the way, truth, and life, and no one comes to God except through Him.

Joe excused himself for a while. It was Saturday October 17. He was out walking and exploring. He was soul searching and looking at things. He smiled at kids playing with their parents and having true fun. He walked by churches slowly. He walked by Lucy's new home. He walked by the shop. He thought and thought of his life. He had much success, and failure. He felt his life was worthless at times. He felt he had messed his life up. He felt bad for hurting his family as much as he did. He felt he had ruined many relationships. He knew Sally had believed and come to Jesus before her tragic death. He did not understand why God had taken her and her fiancé who loved Jesus. But he had heard 400 people came to Jesus as a result. Peopled came to Jesus and they would have been very happy. God had saved many people who were terrible sinners. He decided to come to Jesus once and for all and this time for real. He thought he would finally have never ending peace that would bring him real true happiness at last.

Joe thought back to his parents. In every house, they had a prayer/Bible study room. It had lots of Bibles and Christian books and Adventures in Odyssey albums and Christian help books. It had a table and desk. And it was sound proof so people could spend time alone in prayer and reading with God without distractions from the outside of the room. They had it in each of their homes, and people loved the little room. People would sign up for times inside the room.

Joe decided there was only one place he could accept Jesus. And there were only a few people he could pray with to accept Jesus. He called Lauren and Mark and asked them to meet him and their parent's home. He went there and wanted to go into Bible/prayer room. He arrived a little after 3:00, and his parents and Lauren and Mark were sitting in the front den when he walked in.

He told him he had made a decision. He told them he had been doing a lot of thinking, He apologized for hurting them so much and all his rebellion. He said he knew he had been a terrible son and brother and there was a lot of stuff he regretted a lot. He told them he was doing a lot of soul searching and looking at his life and was not happy when he looked. He said it was like looking into a mirror, and not liking what you see there. And that is how he felt, empty inside.

"I have messed up my life so much. I could have been a Christian and had a great ministry and wife and kids who were always with me. I have goofed in so many ways. But I have learned. I want to go with ya'll to the prayer room and accept Jesus into my life. I want to become a true Christian and I want to start living my life for Jesus and I want to be better."

They were very overjoyed. They started crying. They were so happy. They told him they had been waiting years to hear him say that. They were had never given up on him, and had been praying daily. They were glad he was coming to the Lord, and would never regret it. They encouraged him and held him. They told him how great this way, and they would never forget this day.

Lauren talked to him between tears. "Well, big bro, this is it. You have always meant the world to me. Even when you embarrassed me and my friends. Even when you were the biggest jerk in the world and were mean and rude to me. I always loved you. I still believe you are the best brother. We had so much fun as kids, and we were a great team. You are still young. You are 31. You can still do wonders for God and serve Him and be the man for you. I believe in you, big bro. You will do awesome things for Jesus, and you will still accomplish much for Him and in your life. Congrats on the best decision you will ever make. This is one for all time, the one that will decide eternity. And one day you will be in Heaven. Awesome."

His mom told him how much she loved him and she knew one day he would tell her that. She said she had a dream the night before God would have told her that would be the day. She had known it and shared it with Jack. They had been in a good day all day long.

His dad spoke next. He could not even talk at first, he was so moved. He was crying. "Son, I love you so very much. You are my only son. I want you in Heaven with me. I am so happy to see you turn your life over to Jesus. You are making an excellent decision. Like Lauren said, it is the best decision you could ever make. You will be in Heaven now when you die.

They started kissing and hugging him. They did it without shame. After a few minutes, they went to the Prayer room and they all knelt. This is where Joe decided to become a Christian, in the prayer room with his parents and sister and brother in law.

"Lord Jesus, I come to you. I am a horrible sinner. I am the worst sinner possible. I have rebelled and rejected you. I have sinned at every turn. I am not worthy of you, you are the perfect only true God. I have cursed your name. I have been a drunk and drug addict. I have broken my family's hearts again and again. I am worthy of hell. I deserve hell. But o, Jesus, I am turning to you. I need you. I am broken and humbled before you. I need you in my life. I want you in my life. Please come into my heart, Jesus. I want you to change my life. I want you to help me. Please come into my life. I accept you as my Savior. I need you. I cannot live without you. I am empty inside. I am hopeless. I am the most evil man. Jesus, you are the way, the truth, and the life. You are the only way I can get to Heaven. Lord Jesus thank you for dying for me. Thank you for dying on the cross for me. Thank you for raising me from the dead. Thanks for being such an awesome God. I now know you are the only true God. Please forgive me of my sins. I am not worthy of your love, so thanks. Thanks for loving me and never giving up on me. I love my family. Thanks for the awesome family. They love me and never gave up on me. They are like you. Most people would have given up on me. But they prayed for me. They helped me. Thank you Jesus. Now, Lord please be my Savior. Please be Lord of my life and help me to be better and to live for you in all that I do. I want you to be in my heart. Please, please come and save me. In Jesus' name, Amen."

And Joe Allen had finally become a Christian. He had quit running and rebelling and had finally turned his life over to Jesus Christ. His life would never be the same, it would be awesome now, and it would just be getting better and better. Joe was a new creation.

Chapter 7
The Aftermath

Instantly, he felt instant peace. He felt the peace rush all over him. He laughed. His family was crying and laughing and hugging and kissing him. They were telling him how much they loved him and how much God loved him. They told him the angels in Heaven were rejoicing and praising God. They told him how proud of were of Him and how much this was awesome .They had waited and prayed for this day for so many years. It was one of the happiest days of their lives.

Joe called Lucy and told her of his decision. She was expecting it. She cussed him out. She had the divorce papers all ready for him. If he ever got saved, she would divorce him. She called him scum and a pig and filthy things about him and God. She never wanted to see him again and hoped he died. She said she hoped he rotted and to never bother him again, their relationship was over forever. She never wanted anything to do with him again, and he could be with his God.

Joe was very saddened by all this, but of course he had been expecting it. He had known for years Lucy was an atheist and was not about to change and become a God believer. He would miss her, but felt they had fought too much and had fallen out of love. And now he would be going through a second divorce. He felt some things were for the best considering some stuff. With all the circumstances about what they believed and now lived their lives, it seemed they could never be friends again. Joe and his family would pray for Lucy every day God would change her heart and bring her to Him. Joe had been saved, so they believed Lucy could one day be saved and be a Christian as well.

Joe told his entire family the good news. He started going to all the church events. He started reading the Bible and really getting into it. He was getting into the Christian faith. He was devouring everything he could. He was listening to Christian radio and preachers again. He was reading Christian books by famous authors. He spoke to few churches and area ministries and shared his faith. Youth events were packed, when he spoke. He went to a few places in Georgia and the Carolina's. He returned to the places he used to live and preached for a while. He became popular. He was a kind of famous cartoonist. He had become very loved and people had asked for his testimony. He was always a great speaker and preacher, and was even coming better now. His people person skills were back. He was sought after.

Joe usually gave the same talks. He spoke of all that had happened to his life. He told of how he acted like a Christian and he said he said and did the right things. "I was just showing off. I did not really believe. I wanted to show off and be the best I could be. I could memorize the Bible and say what I needed to say. I wanted people to think I was the very best. I am a great actor, and could pull it off. God gave me talents and drama is one of them. I could be the best actor ever, and I had a lot of people fooled. I thought I was the best ever. I thought I could do anything I wanted to do.

"I went to Christian camps a lot. I loved them. I went to 3

62

Christian camps from age 7 to 15, and had great fun. I loved the friendships and relationships. I was popular. I entered the talent shows and sang and did skits. The counselors trusted me and let me be in charge. As in real life, the people would turn to me and turn to me for advice. I was the athlete around camp. People would pick me for the teams at a young age. Everyone wanted to be my friend. I was considered the man by others. I could get my Bible verse memory patches. I would speak to others for Jesus. I stopped going to camp when I turned against God when I was 15 and 16. I gave it all up. I gave up on a lot of things I now regret. I wish I could finish up the camp Faith time and do it all again. I could have graduated with my friends and been one of the oldest campers and been a real role model. We would always play the funnest games at camp. We played baseball when people would put their names into a hat and the director would draw them out and boys and girls would hold hands for the game. The Cabin 4 older guys would challenge the staff, and the girls would play volleyball. We played cool games and had fun times. We won the grand prize a few times. We had great Christian music and great speakers. The best preachers came and shared. The counselors were the best, especially Mr. Cal and his wife. They have been doing it 40 years. The director truly cared for all. A tornado struck in 1991, and it was rebuilt better than ever. It was a truly awesome beautiful place. They do a wonderful place. They preach the Gospel and truly care for everyone and preach the truth. It is the best camp out there. I had the best of experiences and times there and I messed it all up and it is my own fault. I made the best friends for a lifetime. I have a photo album full of great photos.

"I loved them and now am going to go back there every summer during the 2 Teen weeks and help others and be a counselor. They say they are going to be more than glad to welcome me back. I am excited I can go back and work there again. It is truly a wonderful camp. I want to help others and help them know of Jesus and show them how they can know Him and have a relationship with Him as well. I hope I can make an impact. I want to be for them as others were for me.

"My family loved me so much. They never gave up on me. They prayed for me every day. They did this for me so much. I loved my sister. We played all kinds of cool games with her. I even played with her dolls. We were best friends. We tried to out gross each other. We played the funniest games. She was the best older sister I could ever have. We sang together. We pretended to preach and be on the radio together. We listened to Stories of Great Christians every day and pretended they were about us and our family. We helped others and they loved us. She shared with me. She taught me a lot. She was awesome. She was my hero. So was my grandpa. I never wanted to disappoint him. He died before I turned rebellious, but I was the biggest jerk to Lauren. I cussed her out and made her cry a lot. I don't know how she loved me still, if not for God she would have given up on me and hated me. I almost ruined our relationship. I was terrible to her. I was the worst brother to her at times. I was evil to her. O, I wish I could go back and do all that again. I would go back to change and never done all I had done. I would have been the sweetest guy and helped her always. I am glad I am back now. She forgave me and I am glad she did. She accepted me and took me back. Mark and her are a happily married couple with 3 kids and have the best marriage and they love each other so much. She teaches her kids, 2 girls and a boy, like me, just like our parents taught us. Sure, her kids can be gross and rowdy like us, but only in private. She teachers her kids the best values just like our parents did.

"Our parents taught us obedience. They taught us to respect others. They taught us to have love for everyone. We had to look both ways before crossing the street. We got away from strangers. We only watched the best TV shows. We read Bible and prayed together every day. We were in church a lot. We were always taught of Jesus and of God. We were taught how to get to Heaven. They told us to stay close by. They were the best parents ever. They showed us how to have pure, clean fun. And I turned my back on them. I disrespected them I showed them hate. I was terrible. I regret the way I treated them. Like Lauren and God, they never turned their backs on me. They prayed for me every day as well. My parents are so Godly. I don't know how I could treat them like I did. I wish I could do it all over again.

"Now, my parents were a lot like me. They had sex before marriage with others. They conceived Lauren out of wedlock. They let it be known they could never judge me. They loved me unconditionally. They never turned their backs on me. They loved me always. They are the best. They love God with all their hearts and obey Him and want to serve Him in all they do. People love and respect them and want them to help them. They are such awesome people and I love them so much."

He always talked of his marriages and kids and how they failed. He spoke of how he could never find true happiness no matter what He tried. He told them all the wrong things he had tried. He spoke how he did bad things and it was stupid.

"Don't learn the hard way, people. Learn from my mistakes. God had shown me this way so I can help others and ya'll can avoid what I did. Live for Jesus and serve Him in all you do. Keep your eyes focused on Him. Love Him Love others. Keep Him # 1 in your life. Serve Him in all I do. I challenge you to follow Him. Forget about being made fun of, ignore them. Accept Jesus. It will be worth it. My life before was trash. Avoid it. Please don't know as I did. Please don't turn to sex, drinking, drugs, and money, power. I had it all in one hand. But I was empty inside. God will forgive your sins. All of us sin and make mistakes. Don't feel God won't forgive you. If God forgives me and Sally and others, He will forgive anyone. Turn to Him and He will accept and forgive Him and be Lord of your lives and awesome things will happen in your life."

He got many standing ovations. People loved to hear him preach and share his testimony. Many people accepted Jesus. People cried during his talks. He became well known around the South. He was very popular with schools and churches. He took Fridays-Sundays off to speak. He still worked, but did his

65

speaking on the weekends. He started tithing 20 % of his paychecks to make up for when he never tithed. He gave to area charities and volunteered at night some. He took Bible college correspondence courses and got a Bible certificate online from Ivy Bible College. He took many Bible lessons online and in the mail. He learned a lot and was soaking it all in. He was becoming a Christian leader at long last. He was memorizing the Bible, this time for real and had much Bible knowledge and was working hard to tell others what He was leaning. He especially loved FCA events, and meeting famous Christian athletes. He urged people not to make athletics their God as he had. He had then given up on it and then lost it all. They could lose it overnight as well. He met the Christian Atlanta Braves and other professional and college Christian athletes.

Over the next 2 years, from 2009-2011 things went the same. The divorce was final in March 2010. Lucy moved to Texas, and they never saw each other again. Luke visited every June and first 2 weeks of July. He loved his son. He and Lucy talked on phone 3 times about stuff and she would always hate him for the rest of her life. She would never accept Jesus, and die an atheist. She thought Joe was a big fool, and hated him more than anyone else. She was glad she got her wish to never see him again.

Joe had quit doing the comic strip in 2005 when they moved to Monk. He considered bringing it back as a Christian comic book and thought that may be cool. He had also written 2 books with strips, and they had made him money set for a while. He wrote a best selling book about his conversion, it was even # 1 on Christian and the New York times bestseller list for a few weeks.

He took summer 2010 and appeared in Christian talk shows. He shared if was worth it in some ways if he could prevent others from making the same mistakes. He had an internet site to share his faith and it was very popular. He had many online friends, and many would sign his guest book. He was like he was as a boy again. His jokes and stories were very popular. He was sought out for advice. Many people would ask him to pray for them. He gave much advice and help to others. People would challenge him to games and contests and card games. He was good. Teenage girls loved him. He was getting invitations to proms and banquets as the guest of honor. He spoke at camps and was a counselor at Camp Faith Time teen weeks in July. He also helped with games and music. He attended Monday night classes at an Augusta Bible school for lay people. He became an elder at a local Presbyterian Church of America church there in Monk. He co-hosted a local radio show on Fridays. In fall 2010, he only spoke on Saturdays and Sundays to not prevent his work at the store. He was eating and drinking better now.

He made great Christian friends. He taught a Bible study after attending some and learning. He dated Megan some, but they were more friends. She married a local dentist named Willy Wright. 2 of his partners became Christians. He told the most awesome stories. People could listen to him for life. He helped counsel many people. He considered people his best friends. He was going strong for the Lord. He taught a local Christian drama team that did skits and plays on Friday nights. His skits and plays were a lot of fun. Everyone loved them, and laughed a lot and cried some as well.

He was in great shape. He ate good and exercised a lot. He drank good drinks. He did not eat much fat. He ran 2 miles every morning and lifted weights. He watched only good TV shows. He watched the Braves a lot. He went to 3 games every month. He met the players and loved that. He spoke at Augusta minor league games on Sundays and they loved him. He helped some players come to know God. He was very popular. He attended home games a lot and people would want to sit near him. He played sports with the kids and had great fun with them. He could still throw a football over 30 yards and make baskets from the other side of the court. His travel was cut less and less. Starting in January 2011, he only spoke at 2 churches a month, every other Sunday. His responsibilities were increasing in Monk.

He loved sending emails and letters in mail. He would buy 10 books of stamps at a time and write to people all over. People were writing to him and asking for advice and help. He would help them the best he could. He loved letters. People loved the personal letters he would send back. He would write to teens the most, and all the girls thought he was the cutest, sweetest, and funniest man with the most awesome stories. He was a great letter writer, and enclosed pictures of himself. The people would enclose pictures of them to match a face with a name. Joe loved this.

In 2012, he spoke in Dillin, Alabama. A girl named Michelle Marks heard him speak. She wrote him a letter, and he wrote her back. They just briefly met. That was that for now. Later, it would be more. But he got so many letters she was just one more teen to him.

In January 2011, he started working at the store less. He was set in money for a while. He volunteered at Habitat for Humanity and Soup Kitchen. He only worked at the store 2 days a week, Tuesday and Wednesdays. He still liked it ok. He did the radio show.

In May 2011, 3 friends moved to Strawberry, Mississippi where they were from. They opened up a Habitat for Humanity there and opened a radio station. After thinking and praying about it for 2 weeks, Joe moved there as well in July.

Chapter 8
Mississippi

Joe moved to Strawberry, Mississippi in 2011. He went with Tom and Katie, Art and Amanda, and Jim and Leslie. They were excited about all they would be doing. They started a new Habitat for Humanity after 3 months and the soup kitchen was at the church across the street. They did the Christian radio show from 6-8 on weekdays. They were very popular. They discussed current events, played Christian music, people called in and asked questions, and the show got big ratings. They also did local Strawberry Christian School athletic events like baseball, football, basketball, soccer, and volleyball. People from all over town would listen in and it became so popular it was moved to 5-8 after just 6 months. They got more fan mail than anyone. They did funny skits and jokes and stories on the radio. Joe went to churches and schools and shared his testimony again. He became very popular here as well. He joined a local PCA church and helped teach Junior high Sunday School and Clubs on Sunday nights. He enjoyed teaching and the students loved him and he enjoyed sharing. They thought he was interesting and loved his jokes and stories. A lot of times, Sunday school was divided between boys and girls. 2 times a month, it was like that. And thanks to Joe, it was now both guys and girls together 2 times a month instead of just the first Sunday of the month. Joe preached and filled in for area churches 2 Sunday nights a week, and his helped teacher Bob would fill on for him instead.

Joe was loving living there. He attended a lot of home games for the Christian school, and not just because he was the DJ. He enjoyed high school sports. He encouraged them and gave them tips. He told them not to quit like he did. He helped them in new ways. The coaches would let them coach in practice some and he loved it. He loved making the long shots. He had a lot of fun. He was good at 3 pointers and foul shots. They played horse and 21.

He dated a teacher named Nancy for 3 months, but it did not work out. He tried dating Becky from the station, who was a lot like Lauren in a lot of ways for 2 months, and it did not work out. They remained friends an co workers without any problems. He dated Ashley from the YMCA some, but she moved to South Dakota to go to school. So dating was not going as well as he had hoped, but things were still good. He was making lots of good friends and ministry was good.

He was still popular with letters. He published 2 books to help teens. He published letters with permission, and names and locations were changed, with a few facts. He gave good advice, as he had very good insight. He was a good counselor, and helped many people with problems. He wrote an advice column on his web page, and updated it 3 times weekly himself. He liked it better that way. He also would help people on the radio from 7:15-7:40 and talked to people after the show on the phone.

The Habitat for Humanity restore was very popular. People were bringing in many things from home they did not use anymore. People loved the low prices and the store was selling out of clothes and furniture in a hurry. They got some book and electronics and housebound appliances. They bought a store room next door and got a truck to buy things from people's homes. They would take some things to some people's homes as well. They got volunteers from the community to help out. Some people did community service there when they got in trouble with the police. The store was packed at times. They had 2 managers, 1 employee, and 16 volunteers at various times. They were thankful. It was good. They had specials every one in a while. People would drop off stuff when they did not need it, so it could be sold.

The other Habitat was good. They built homes for poor people. A national charity sent them ten million dollars. They designed a local neighborhood of 55 homes and 2 pools and they were all Habitat homes. College students would help, especially on breaks. It took 1 ½ years to finish the Merrymont project. It was very popular, and many poor people moved in. They were modest 3 bed 2 bath homes, nothing too fancy. They had back and front yards, which people loved.

Joe helped take the youth group to different places every other Saturday, They went to Atlanta and Six Flags or Braves games or Hawks. They saw Mississippi and Mississippi State football games. They witnessed in New Orleans. They went swimming or a water park or theme park. One time they went tubing down a river. They went bowling and roller skating and to see good movies. They hung out at the church or at people's homes. They played the funnest games. Joe taught them the games he and Lauren had invented as kids. They had lots of fun. Of course, the real youth pastor and his assistant were in charge. Joe just helped. They loved Scavenger games the most. They played it once a month. They also loved Capture the Flag and Find the Christians, a game his youth director had made up in Carters. Joe and the people invented some games too. He only spoke to the group every once in a while, and sat on the sidelines or in the back.

Joe was thinking seriously about Bible college. He was

thinking about doing the whole thing by correspondence. He was also thinking about having it and attending a real college for 4 years. He tried writing Ivy Bible College in South Carolina where Lauren had gone. He wrote Oakley Bible College in Virginia, Fork Bible College in Florida, Millwood Bible College in far off Pennsylvania, and Marietta Christian College right there in Mississippi. He had spent so many years in Hammonds, even with his family there, he needed a new life. Millwood was very good, but was just too far away. He wrote to about 10 colleges and got the information and sat down and looked and pondered and prayed about it.

Joe continued to stay in good health. He swam and lifted weights and ran daily. He walked a lot as well. He joined the local gym. He went bowling every Saturday morning and raised his average from 96 to 111 in the 2 years. He was very excited about this. He also averaged more strikes. He would find stray dogs and take them in and put up posters until the owner found them. The longest he kept one was a bulldog he named Harry that was really named Benny. He had him for 2 months.

Joe saw his daughters some during the year. He enjoyed that. He went home 1 weekend per month to see the family. He enjoyed the 5 weeks during the summer and 3 weekends a year he saw his son Luke. He heard Lucy badmouthed him to everyone.

Joe took in a roommate for 6 months in 2012. Mike Marshall was a 28 year old widower who wanted to go to Bible college as well. He was going to a small school in Kentucky and was going to attend in Fall 2014. He was working 2 jobs in the meantime and saving up money. He was a good guy who lived out of the bedroom and was not messy. He was very nice and attended the same church as Joe. They lived in a 3 bedroom 2 bathroom house on Old River Road right near the Baptist church on the outskirts of town. Joe had fallen in love with the house the first time he had seen it and knew he wanted to live there one day. At first, he had been living with the youth director and then the pastor. He moved after being in town for

3 months and very much enjoyed living in his own home again. Having someone else share half the living expenses was great. Mike had a girlfriend named Brooke. Joe dated a couple of girls named Mandy and Nicole. They would watch DVDS and movies every Tuesday and Thursday nights together in the living room. Sometimes, they would watch regular TV. They would go to the movie theater every Friday night and enjoyed the movies. Mike dated the same women for a long time, and they would marry in 2014 and have 6 kids. Joe could never date a woman more than a month, there was just not any magic there, and things just did not work out in a romantic sense.

In December 2012, Joe decided to go to Ivy Bible College. He would start in August 2012. He used to live in Ivy, and that is where Lauren went. She met her husband Mark there. Joe wanted to meet his wife there. He had prayed for his future wife every day since December 2011. He read his Bible and prayed daily, and knew he was ready for Bible college. He wanted to be surrounded by Christian leaders and fellowship and be more equipped and trained in the ministry. He was well saved in money and was ready to go. He would miss it there, he would only be there 2 years, but he wanted to go to Bible college. And there were the 3 couples and church leaders to run things smoothly and make it a success.

Joe wrote 3 books while he was in Mississippi. One was a children's book called Roger, Roger, and Roger. It was about 3 best friends named Roger at a farm. It was a pig, a chicken, and a horse. Someone named Mary Beth Cook drew the pictures. Joe was a good artist, but never had all the time. It was a good book and sold well around the country. He also wrote a partial autobiography on all God had brought him through. He changed all the names and changed around the facts and added stuff and combined people. He talked about all that God had brought him through. It was a best seller as well. If he had wanted, he could have been a traveling evangelist traveling across the country sharing his stories. He would love that, but wanted to go to Bible college first. He felt he wanted that degree he had earned and would give him more opportunities. He wanted to teach and coach and work at a church and a degree would give him those chances.

The third book was about Christians dealing with divorce. He talked about some of his own experiences. It too was a best seller. He changed some stuff again, but Lucy hated him all the more. With 3 best seller books, he was done writing for a while and was more famous now. He was even getting autograph requests from around the nation and felt he was like a famous movie star or athlete or musician. Sometimes he was treated like one, and did not know what to do. Tourists would drive by his house at times just to see where he lived. He would put a gate around his house eventually.

In April, for spring break, the family went to the Grand Canyon in Arizona. Most had never been before. They stayed for 4 nights. It was an awesome trip and everyone was very glad they had gone. Joe had always read of the Grand Canyon and seen pictures, but this was majestic. Everyone took 2 rolls of film and videotaped it so they could always remember what a great time they had there. Joe did not want to leave. Lauren's kids loved it the most and they pretended to be cowboys. It really was an awesome trip.

Life returned to normal in Strawberry in a hurry. Joe felt the ministries were doing awesome for people. The soup kitchen was helping to feed people who needed food. The people also shopped at Habitat. It was still a crowded store at times and was donated to by people from around the state. They were both very popular and everyone was glad. The radio show had the highest ratings on the station, and one of the 5 highest in the area from any radio station. The church had grown as well, especially in the youth department. More teens and kids who did not attend church before they arrived were now attending the church and some became Christians and there was much rejoicing about this of course.

Joe begun to receive letters from the 125 people who would attend Ivy Bible College that fall as freshmen. They told him about themselves and he wrote back. They wanted to kind of know him before they went so they would not be total strangers.

Mike lived with 3 other guys now. But Joe and he and Brooke still hung out some. They would still watch movies on TV and DVD and at the theater some. Joe had a roommate named Scott in Spring 2013 who was a college student and worked at a restaurant and was single. He left early in the mornings and came home late at night and just needed a place to live. He attended the local junior college and was getting an associates degree in mechanical engineering. He was a Christian who had always lived in Mississippi or Alabama. He was a great guy, but Joe did not see him that much as he was so busy.

In addition to the books, Joe wrote his Sunday cartoon strip during the 2 years he was in Strawberry. It was in 300 newspapers and was popular again. Joe planned to end it when he went to Bible college again, too much time studying and working some. The head of the computer lab promised him a job there. He was excited about working in a Christian college computer lab and was preparing. His colorful characters in the strip made them very much loved, and he would turn them into a book after he finished. People were sad his strip would end, but understood about him going to Bible college.

Joe liked getting together with his family every month. He spent the summer with Luke. His daughters came to visit him for 3 of those weeks. He enjoyed spending time with them all. The girls were teens now and in college. They attended a college in North Carolina and both had boyfriends and were popular. They would soon be 19. Luke was almost 10. He was liking girls now and even had a little girlfriend. He did not like his half sisters teasing him about this. His mom was very anti God in a lot of ways. It was really bad ever since her teen brother was killed. And when her husband turned to God she was mad. She never took Luke to church and never let him learn of God around the house. The friends he had taught him some. His dad taught him some. He believed in God, and had a Bible he read away from the house. He would never ever tell

75

his mom that of course. There was a few times he did not like his mom that much because of her beliefs. Anyways, Joe and his children spent a lot of time together and went places and saw things and met people. They thought it was really cool that their dad had become famous now. They ate ice cream and pizza and went out and watched DVDS and went to the theater. They played games and acted silly at times. The girls felt they were too mature and old for some stuff. They went to the annual 4th of July bash with the whole family and had a good time. And then they went back to their own home and Joe was thankful for the time he spent with them.

When Joe left for Ivy Bible College in August, he was leaving everything in good hands. The ministries were popular and helping many. Many had homes now. The radio show was heard in a lot of Christian stations around Mississippi and Alabama and Louisiana. Lucy could hear if she wanted, but she had no desire. The church was growing. The church and station had a good bye party for him at the local college gym. 3,000 people came and said goodbye. Joe spent time with all his close friends before going. He left the town in awesome shape. The party touched him. He felt loved. He had only been there 2 years, yet still felt they cared for and loved him, and he loved them. They gave him goodbye presents. Someone had copied down all his stories and jokes and was going to turn it into a book. It touched Joe very much. They all helped him pack and said goodbye to him on Monday morning and he headed to a new challenge at Ivy Bible College.

Chapter 9
Bible College

Joe arrived at Ivy Bible College in August 2013. He decided to be a freshman and attend all 4 years with the same class. At 35, he was almost twice as old as most of them. The 2nd oldest freshman was 26, and he was the 5th youngest underclassman. He was going to live in a dorm room, but by himself. He left a lot of stuff at the attic of his home in Hammonds. It was a small home in his parent's big back yard. He wanted to be in the middle of things at campus and be a mentor and help for the guys. He arrived in time for Welcome weekend all the activities that would take place. There was going to be speakers, teams and games played, tours, picnic, barbecue dinner, assemblies. They divided into family groups and shared of their lives. They started meeting new friends. The speakers spoke of Ivy Bible college and all that went with it. They had a drop in at the homes of the President, dean of college, and dean of students. The dean of men and women spoke to the groups individually. The games and activities they did was a lot of fun.

They arrived on Thursday and Monday was when all the other students started arriving. Registration was Tuesday and Wednesday. Classes started on Thursday. Joe had 50 total hours but was going to be registered as a freshman. He would take 3-4 classes a semester and do less and finish in 4 years like most people. He had a good welcome weekend. He had 3 guys and 4 girls in the group. Juniors named Abe and Katherine were the leaders. One day, they would get married. The guys were Michael, Tom, and Frank. The girls were Anne, Alicia, Leslie, and Destiny. They became close. Many people came and met Joe. He was famous. They had written each other letters.

It was all good. Joe met all the guys on his hall. He lived in Freedom Dorm Hall 3. There were 20 guys on the Hall. The RA was named Aldan Kellen. He was a 22 year old senior from Lansing. The guys all seemed to be good solid guys and Joe was excited to be there. He met them all Friday and helped them move in. He met the parents as well. Friday and Saturday nights he shared for them all and they had hall meetings. Everyone stayed up late. He said he would there for all of them at any time.

Joe was making lots of good friends in a hurry. The girls all thought he was cute and like a father figure, as did some guys. The girls were in love with him right away. He was surrounded by people in chapel and meetings and the school cafeteria. He was already very popular. He told his stories and jokes and stuff and people were laughing and carrying on. He was considered the life of the party. People already told him they were gonna seek him out and get advice, and he said great.

He registered for 4 classes that 1st semester. He would have 12 hours, including a field education elective. He would be doing evangelism to young boys in the Ivy area. He would be on team with 3 other guys. He was excited about that. He would have 3 classes on Monday Wednesday and Thursday each. The other course would be Tuesday and Thursday. His major would be Christian Education. He had taken most of beginning Bible courses and early electives like English and science and math out of the way, and he was very excited about this of course. He loved the Christian Education professors and the program and courses. He wanted to take a few youth classes as well, as he wanted to work with youth. He had always enjoyed it and wanted to help then avoid the mistakes he had made in the past. He showed them good stuff when he worked with them. He listened intently in class and took very good notes he studied hard.

Joe clicked with a girl named Lauren, ironically enough. She was a 21 year old senior set to graduate in May with a minor in Christian Education and a major in counseling. They dated for over 2 months before deciding just to be friends in November. They did enjoy it for a while. She was from Ivy, and her family loved him, but weren't thrilled with the age difference and the fact she was only 2 years older than his twin daughters. They enjoyed having devotions together, playing putt putt, bowling, car rides, and seeing movies with everyone else on campus. Well, about 50-60 people would gather and watch movies somewhere on campus, and they enjoyed this. The weekends were the most popular for this. Lauren even went home to meet his family one weekend in October. She got along with the other Lauren, even if they were complete opposites and did not have too much in common. Lauren Townsend did not think his sister's talents were that great. She was a pretty blonde and had 2 younger sisters, 14 and 12. Her brothers were 26 and 10. They were also a close knit family. They had a good breakup, and remained friends. Lauren would get back together with her old high school/college boyfriend Ben Brown. They would also eventually marry in January 2014. Joe would be in the wedding. The couple was married 44 years and had 3 kids, 2 boys and a girl, and 8 grandchildren.

The fall semester 2013 went very well. Joe loved his job in the computer lab. He loved working with computers and with the students. He always had extra desks and computer paper he bought with his own money. People had to constantly save papers incase the power went out. Joe had signs saying to save every other line and every paragraph and every pause. Joe was a great help to many people. He worked 4 days a week and was in there a lot when he was not working. He did good on all his papers. He was a whiz on the computer. People would come up to him and ask for advice and prayer and help in all areas. Sometimes they would leave for privacy. The other lab workers liked him as well.

Joe did real good in all in classes. He made straight A's in his classes. He was always very smart and it came very easily for him. He did not need to study that much. He was happy he was doing so good. The professors liked him very much and depended on him. He helped them out. He liked doing projects with other guys and working on stuff. He did real good on tests. He did good on the papers. He enjoyed learning in his classes and took part in some discussions.

Joe was a big man in the cafeteria. When it was someone's birthday, he would tap his silverware on the glasses and stand on the chair and call attention. The whole cafeteria would sing happy birthday to the person. Joe was surrounded by people at all times. He spent time with different people each meal. He always had the most interesting things to talk about. He always was very polite with best manners around women. He got men to stand up as women arrived at the table and left. He would even take their trays and dishes to the dish room for them. He would always sit in a table near the cashier and the line.

It was not just the cafeteria and computer lab and movie nights he was popular with people. One weekend a month was Open Dorms at the guy's dorms. Another weekend a month it was at the girl's room. Joe had set his room very clean and had put pictures and notes and emails from the girls for them to see. His room was always very popular on those nights. He was very glad to see all the girls and friends stop by and they visited and talked and had good fellowship. He always visited the girl's room and made them feel special and loved that. He would stop by and see them all at all open dorms.

Joe was big on help and encouragement. He wrote people

encouragement notes a lot. He was always smiling and being nice and happy and greeting people. He would seek out people and tell them he was thinking and praying for them and making sure they were feeling ok. He would buy little presents. He would cheer up the people who were having a bad day. He tried to be friends as many people as possible, but keep just a few as close friends. He had 3 guy friends on his hall he was very close to and confided in. They were Jack, 19, Bobby, 21, and Fred, 20. He was friends with the guys in his group, and they were kind of close, but not like those guys. Joe was a big speaker to the guys on the hall. He would lead dorm devotions and Bible studies and help in meetings. He shared a lot. In early October, he was asked to speak in the men's chapel. They divided the men and women up in chapel 2 times a month on Fridays. Sometimes they had group chapels, Friday was the special chapels with different things. He prepared the week before for this.

" I want to speak to ya'll about a high. People get high on different stuff. We should be getting high on Jesus. I was getting high on the wrong stuff. I was raised in a Christian home, and got far away from it. I thought drugs and alcohol was the answer. I did a lot of drugs. I am surprised it did not mess up with my head. We smoked pot and got hammered once a week. I am also surprised I was never arrested. Well, I was only a drug dealer for a short time. It was not a good time. I thought it would help. It only made things worse. Drinking and taking drugs do not take away your problems. They do not help you feel better. It may give you a high for a while, but it does not last. It messes you up. I tried meth. It was horrible. It is one of the worst things out there. Please never ever do any kinds of drugs. My friends could be just as messed up and high as me. We thought we were at the top of the world. Friday nights seemed to be the greatest.

"One Friday night when I was 30 I realized it was all stupid. My wife and I were temporally separated, one day for real. I woke up on Saturday and felt so sick. Throw up and vomit was all over my bathroom, clothes, floor, and bed. The girl in my bed was a complete stranger to me. I woke up in bed with many women, and did not know some of them. Some I was not close with, and we were in bed together. I still felt sick. It was the worst hangover. My home was a complete mess. People were passed out all over, some without clothes. People I did not even know were all over my house. I did not remember too much about the night before. I remember strip poker and crazy dancing and wild times. It was out of control. I cleaned everything up myself. People left, and no one volunteered to help. It was disgusting. It made me sick again. I had to get some new cleaning products that night because I was running out and had to get new trash bags. I threw away so much trash that night and there was so many beer bottles and cans. It was a mess. I was already looking seriously at my life. And I had never really felt that low. I was at my absolute worst that day. The other worst was when I cussed out my awesome sister and she ran out of the room crying. I decided never to do drugs again. I still drank some and slowly drifted away from some friends. I made sure I did not sleep with strangers.

"A few months later, I was at my parent's house. My cousin's little girl was crying and asking why I was such a mean jerk at times. I was speechless. She was a 6 year old kid with not a mean bone in her whole body. She asked why I liked being drunk better than being with the family. I felt horrible. People told me I embarrassed them when I was drunk. My kinds of high were not right.

"I became saved. I found the answers to true happiness and ended my emptiness. Jesus is the best high, He is the only true high. Jesus is the absolute best. No one or nothing can top Him. Experience Jesus every day. Don't mess with drugs and beer. Sex and money is meaningless if you are just using them and not waiting for marriage. Remember to get high on Jesus, He will never let you down, even in the toughest and hardest of times. Jesus is awesome."

He received much applause for his testimony and talk and challenges. He got a standing ovation, which embarrassed him. He tried to be humble, and told people he was no one special, and was like a lot of people who got saved. He never figured out the fuss about him and thought it was silly. He did appreciate people who told him how much it touched them.

Joe enjoyed that first semester in school. Things were going good. He went home 1 weekend a month. He enjoyed that. He spoke at 1 church a month. He spoke in main chapel in late October. He drew a comic strip for the school newspaper. He had a radio show 7-8 Wednesday nights on the campus radio station. He made a great video for class in October.

Michelle Marks came to visit one Friday in November, 4 days after he and Lauren broke up. She would come in the spring after a semester of junior college. Joe remembered writing her and getting her letters. She was hoping they could be friends and hang out some. He could never forget her name, his daughter Michelle was a year older than her. He promised he would see her that spring and they could be friends and hang out and all that good stuff. She was glad. She had a crush.

Joe helped a lot of guys. He helped disciple some of the younger guys. He led a Bible study for guys every week. He helped in worship every Sunday night when the college students got together. He knew how to play the guitar some and sing pretty good. He helped mentor guys on the hall. He tried to be a good role model. He prayed for those who needed it. He helped people with their schoolwork and papers. He gave good tips. He worked patiently and taught new skills.

He did the same with the boys. He helped them in every way possible. He helped in school and advice. He decided to do this all 4 years. He helped minister to the boys in a poor housing project. A lot of students helped here and were a blessing to the people there. They played games and had lessons and snacks. The people loved seeing them come there. Joe did his skits and jokes.

Joe finished up his first semester and went home for Christmas. The whole family had a good time together and it was some good holidays. Joe was loved again. Lauren always silence the room when it was time to. It shocked people at first and the younger kids always giggled. They had presents and good times and good food and fellowship and Bible reading. Joe was there over New Years and it was a good holiday. Joe was glad his family was so close. And then he went back in January.

Joe was going to take 3 classes and 10 hours this time. One was going to be really challenging, but taught by the most popular professor Dr. Donald Cummings. He had served as assistant dean of the college for 2 years, and interim dean of college, men, and students for one year each. But on the most part, he was just a professor to spend more time on classes and with his students. He had been in the Bible department 36 years, and he was now 69. He would keep on until he was 77. He was well loved and eventually had the Bible department building named after him after 44 years of faithful service. Joe looked up to him, but could not have him for an advisor since he had a different major.

His advisor was the head of the Christian Education. Dr. Tom Harley had spent 22 years in churches with youth, missions, Christian Ed, preaching, and worship. He was in his sixth year at Ivy Bible College, and second as chairman. Joe became close to him as well.

Joe sought out Michelle on her 1st day as a student. He gave her a huge bear hug and welcomed her to campus and helped her move in. Her parents were glad an older famous man would watch out for her and make sure she was ok. They did not live that far away. He again promised to be her friend and spend time with her. They had a good talk. There were only a few new students moving in that spring. Joe helped a few girls and around 6 guys and talked to them all.

Joe had become close to a 32 year old junior named Barry as school wrapped up last December. He was the 4th close friend of Joe's. He too was an older student. He had been involved in drugs and spent 3 years in jail when he was 19 for drunk driving and causing an accident and sexual harassment of a couple of 17 year old girls. He was 21 and in prison when he was saved and 22 when he was released. He had gotten involved in Bible and prayer and ministries. He worked at restaurants. He got his GED when he was 28 when people told him it would be awesome for him and help him. He started at Ivy Bible College when he was 29, and only had to travel 12 minutes from his home. He had a nice setup in his parent's basement with a bedroom, den, and little kitchen. He had a full entrainment system, and Joe hung out some. It had always been really popular with people, and he had lived down there since he was 13, except when he was in jail. He had led his family to God, and they all went to church together. He and Joe became close and helped each other. They read the Bible and prayed together and hung out some. They went on double dates some as well.

Joe was walking around campus a lot. He had a pair of headphones. He would walk 3 miles a day. He would listen to music and Adventures in Odyssey episodes. He always liked trying to stay in top good shape. He took pride in this fact and worked out in the gym weight room 3 times a week. He shot at least 200 shots of basketball every day, and was pretty good again.

Joe went out with a few girls. Only some were in late 20s and 30s, and all were married. He dated some girls some just as friends. He even dated a blind girl named Sherry some. She had Seeing Eye dog. She was a lot of fun. His friend Dave dated a girl named Brooke. They would always be there for movie nights. Joe would always invite a different girl. He was not a pimp or player; he just liked spending time with them as friends, no commitment. It was more fun that way. They loved the attention and little presents. Joe took place in the talent shows and coffee house things. He and Dave did a fun skit when 2 people played 5 characters, including 2 women. People loved it and they won 3rd place. First and second went to serious Christian singing. One time, Lauren and her kids and Joe had their fun. People could not believe them, they thought it was hilarious. They did a skit as well. These nights were always popular. Sometimes, Joe would name all the World Series winners since 1950 or all the Super Bowls winners ever and people were amazed.

Joe's friend's book was published. It was all about Joe and his stories and jokes. It sold out on campus in 2 days the first time, and 1 day when it came back. It was # 1 on the Christian book seller's book for 3 months, and the top 10 on New York Times for 6 weeks. Joe was glad for his friend, and humbled by all that. People were always telling him how much they enjoyed that book as well as the ones Joe had written himself. He thanked them and signed lots of books for people.

Spring 2014 was very good for Joe and people. He went out with some girls. Michelle's family thought he was too old to be her boyfriend for a few years. But they became good buddies. She went home 2 times a month. He visited her one weekend. He realized his dream had been the day she was born. They laughed about that and wondered about that. He dated a girl named Nancy for 3 weeks, but things did not work out that way. He started dating a girl named Karen in May. She was from Florida, and would work at a ranch back home for the summer. They promised to keep in touch.

Joe helped lead 6 boys at the housing project to the Lord. He helped a mentally challenged man named Bobby and gave him rides and food and drinks. He ministered to the adults as well. He and Joe Ford and Cheryl visited a woman named Denise there. He and Dave later went back and saw her some. She was dating Bobby some. Joe loved the boys and played football and basketball with them and helped mentor them. Their grades in school were going good. They were doing better in sports. They were cussing less and being nicer to their moms and sisters. The girls were making progress with the younger girls as well. The other guys loved this work as well. It was a real good ministry and it was great. Joe loved it Joe finished up his freshmen year of college in a good way. He was glad he had come here. He was getting good Bible training. He was learning a lot and was getting good ministry experience. He still helped preach at some churches in the Ivy and Lansing areas.

That summer, Joe helped at the YMCA in Hammonds. He helped coach the teams and was an umpire at some games as well. He was popular with the players and was well loved. The parents all loved him as well. They went 14-2 and won the championship. They would have a big awards show at the end of the summer and had plaques and trophies. It was at Pizza Hut. Everyone got an award and was happy. It was an awesome time. The summer was good. Joe loved the time with his family. They always got together a lot. Joe loved Lauren's kids. They had lots of fun. He saw his kids and spent some quality team with them and he was glad. He saw some friends when he spent 2 weeks in Strawberry, which was nice.

He started his sophomore year that August. He would take 4 courses and his Field Education for 13 hours and he was excited. He had kept in touch with Karen over the summer. She had an awesome experience. She was glad, and so was he. They kept on dating that fall. The other girls were disappointed. They went to movie nights and coffee houses and putt putt and fun park and movies. They had good fellowship. In November, the same day he had broken up with Lauren, he had Karen had an argument. She wanted to go on mission's trip that spring to Indonesia area and take the whole semester off. She decided she wanted to do missions work for a career. He did not. They talked and prayed together a lot the week. They had different perspectives and goals for their lives. They loved and cared for each other deeply. But in late November, right before Thanksgiving break, they broke up. They remained friends the rest of her time there. She would later marry a man she met on the tour that spring and they were missionaries there after she graduated for 40 years. She loved the Lord and the people and served Him for the rest of her life.

Joe was single the rest of the fall semester. He was doing ok. He made all 2 A's and 2 B's. He did well in his courses. He mentored 4 new freshmen guys. He remained close with the other 4 guys and helped them a lot. They would study the Bible and pray together for hours. They helped with the ministry to the boys. They helped many people and were looked up to.

Joe organized games every Sunday afternoon. They played kickball and soccer and flag football. They played the games

Joe had invented. They had a lot of fun. They liked the spy games and Joe won the games. At times they even played kid games like Red Rover, Hide and Go Seek, Tag, and Duck Duck Goose. They were all kids at heart. They had Burger night every Thursday night at the men's dorms. The dean of men would organize it and people loved it. Board games were very popular as well. Some guys who had been punished would help set up and help on food and drinks. It was a very popular night. They would watch Braves games or playoffs or college basketball games on ESPN. The Super Bowl night was always a big deal and everyone gathered for that one. Below the student center was a place with a big screen TV. Cable had come to campus in 2001. Some dorms had basic channels as well. It was all good.

Joe hung with Michelle some, but too much as he dated Karen. He took Michelle out to ice cream right before Christmas break. He preached at her church 4 weeks as they looked for a new preacher. They had a good time. A girl named Becky worked there. She was a college student and had braids some. She was from Alabama and had a strong southern accent. She was the sweetest person alive. She loved her job at Dairy Queen and always did her best at all times and she was popular.

Joe hung out at the Java Station some. He played games and talked to friends. They liked doughnuts and coffee, It was good fellowship.

Joe continued to work in the computer lab and loved it as much as before. He had a note on the door to close the door properly shut. It came open easily and wind came in. The sign remained there for years. Joe got onto monitors for playing music too loud. He helped teach a computer class since the teacher was sick some. He designed new programs and fixed computers when they messed up. He would give people disks and paper if they were running out. He bought 4 new computers for the library. He also bought them 40 new books. He helped many people in the lab.

The spring sophomore year was good too. He had 11 hours

and made 2 A's and 2 B's again. He helped lead more young guys to the Lord. He was interim pastor at an Ivy community church for 2 months. He then helped teach Sunday School and played guitar at Sunday morning worship after the new pastor started. He did not date one girl, but treated them all to meals in the cafeteria. He would have birthday cakes and dinners for them. He was glad to spend time with many people as friends. He helped many guys in the dorm. He stayed all 4 years in the same room and private bathroom, he liked that. He helped his RA's and floor leaders. He still helped with Bible studies and worship. He was a leader on campus. And his 2nd year ended good.

Joe did a 7 week mission trip to Korea that summer. He helped with drama and sports and evangelism. He helped start 2 churches. He worked with youth and children the most. He had a good experience, but did not want to be a career missionary. But he respected the jobs they did very much, and was very thankful for missionaries. He learned a lot there.

Joe spent time with his family of course. He still had been spending time at Camp Faith Time every summer. He loved it. He was counseling, and the kids loved him. He always spent 2 weeks there. They had the funnest weeks. And then it was time to be a junior. Joe spent the time with his family in late August and packed his clothes and went back to IBC.

Joe was happy to be a junior. He would take 3 courses and 10 hours. And from now on, it would be all Christian Education courses. He was going to take one course in children's ministry and one in youth ministry. He had come to love everyone there and spent a lot of time in the CE lounge reading, writing, and talking to many people. They knew where he would be.

Joe dated a musician named Melody for 2 months, but spent most of his junior year hanging out with friends. He helped in the dean of men's office on Thursday mornings, when he had no classes. He wrote a new book which would be published in December. He had kept a diary in Korea, and would share his experiences. He was doing the same thing with

Ivy Bible College. He was excited about sharing his mission trip with the world, and was encouraging others to do the same.

Joe always spoke to incoming students at Welcome weekend. He spoke to guys in more details. He spoke in CE chapels. He spoke at the worship services on Sundays and played his guitar. He had a radio show on the student station on Wednesdays from 7-9. Dave and Brooke helped do it as well. He hosted a music show on the main station heard all over the Carolina's on Tuesday nights from 8-10 and it was very popular. He helped do dramas and helped teach others as well.

Joe also started visiting more people. He visited nursing homes and hospitals. He went in the rooms and spent time with people. He got to know them and minister to the people. His heart went out to the sick kids, especially the ones with cancer. He made them smile and laugh a lot. He gave money to cancer research. He loved the older people's stories from older days. He also even visited prisons and helped minister there and saw some men come to know Jesus and he was happy.

Joe continued to speak and preach at churches. He helped coach intramural teams. He made all A's that year. He sent 3 encouragement notes a day. He prayed for 7 people a day. He sought out sad looking people and helped to cheer them up. He bought presents for people. He helped pay student's tuition by anonymous giving so not to be bigger than anyone. He continued to work hard in the computer lab. He went out with many friends. His bowling average was up to 137. The movie theater people knew him by name and what seats he would sit in. He would show Christian films every Tuesday night in the little chapel and host the nights by introducing the movies and doing the wrap ups. He was on his 2nd photo album and it was full of memories of him serving God and all of his friends he had become close to and helped. His book was a bestseller again. He stayed in good health. He taught people the craziest stuff. He helped lead more people to God. He invented more games. He mentored new guys and it was going good.

Joe had a good junior year. He had only one more year to go. He had taken 3 courses of correspondence over the summers as well. He was going to do his internship at a church at the Grand Canyon South Rim that made him very excited. He said goodbye to all and promised Michelle he would date her more the next school year and she was happy. So was he. They kept in touch all summer with emails, letters, and long phone calls and they could talk for hours.

Joe did an awesome job at the community church at the Grand Canyon. He also washed dishes at a lodge 2 days a week for money. He took 6 rolls of film and met people around the world. He lived with his friend Barry from college in a lodge there. He helped the preacher speak once a month. He taught a Sunday school class and helped in worship. He met interesting people around the world and walked 4 miles a day. He helped with children and adults and loved it. He thought it was the most beautiful place in the world. He witnessed to people there if they wanted to listen. He met several celebrities. He kept a diary there to be published with his Ivy Bible College book. He was glad he had gone there. He also took a trip to Washington DC in August. He worked at the teen camp the last few days of the 2nd week. He was busy before then, and could not do too much. And now he was excited about becoming a senior.

Chapter 10
Michelle

Michelle Katherine Marks was born September 1, 1995. She was the 3rd of 5 kids. Her sister Mary was born in 1991 and brother James in 1993. Kasie was born in 1999 and Bo in 2002. She was a "perfect child" in many ways. Of course, she was a sinner like everyone else. But she was sheltered and never rebelled. She never had smoked, kissed a guy on the lips, drank, had sex, cussed, or gotten into serious trouble. Her family did not have cable until she was 7, and got in for news and sports. Her dad was at Oakley Bible College for 12 years. In 1999, he became a headmaster at a Christian school in Ivy, South Carolina for 4 years. In 2003, he was a principal and coach at a Christian school in Texas. In 2009, he moved to Marshall, South Carolina and taught history and coached 3rd base for the baseball team. Michelle spent her high school days there at Marshall Christian School and was semi-popular. She was a little pretty and was Miss Friendly, Courteous, and Miss

Polite and Cutie Pants at the Junior-Seniors. She dated some, but never really seriously, and was only kissed on the hand or cheek. She wanted her first lip to lip kiss for the wedding day. She was saving herself for her husband in many ways. She was 6th in her class, but there was 12 people, and only 4 guys.

Michelle's parents were like Joe's. They were always polite and had great manners. They were taught to obey and treat adults with respect. She looked both ways before crossing the street, did not talk to strangers, and said "Please, Thank you, Sir and Ma'm, Excuse me, and all the good stuff. She loved to watch Veggie Tales and listen to Adventures in Odyssey. Her family had very album and listened to them on car trips as well. She collected DVDS and CD's. Her dad was well off after doing good in the stock market as a young man, and helping someone invent something. His salaries were very modest. Michelle was very close with her family. She was closer to boys as a girl, and was curious about boys. She was a good soccer player, and watched the Braves games, but was not that big into sports. She collected dolls and toys. She read and wrote a lot. She was not a tom boy. She sang solos and got good parts in musicals. She was an OK actress. She had a good childhood. She never dated anyone more than 2 months, and only had 4 boyfriends and went out with 6 other guys. She attended Christian schools her whole life and church every Sunday. They attended Christian camps, retreats, and conferences. Her family had devotions and Bible reading/prayer/singing hymns an hour a day. They had to read 2 chapters of the Bible daily as they got older. They could only watch Christian TV and read Christian books and Christian music on Sundays. Their parents could be strict, but they loved them so much and the kids were happy. They would help watch the younger kids and did chores around the house.

Michelle knew how to cook some at a young age. She would walk some down the street around the block daily as she got older. She was good at riding her bike. She wrote songs and she would sing them at church or for her friends.

Michelle had several close friends no matter where she

went. She attended pre school and k-4 in Oakley. She spent 4 years in elementary school in Ivy. She 1st spent days at Ivy Bible college, as Ivy Christian School was on the same campus. She graduated from k-5 here. She loved the "big college student dudes" and they became her friend because they would come to the ball games.

In the 3rd grade, they moved to Texas and here she graduated from elementary school in 5th grade and middle school. In the 6 years there, she met many friends. Her best friends were Mandy, Nicole, Brooke, Katie Liz, Tessa and Crystal. Her best guy friends were Dan, Dave, Mikal, Ben and Harley. She played soccer in middle school. She loved going to Six Flags over Texas 6 times a month during the summer. She went 2 Saturdays a month when it was open during the school year. She played the clarinet in 6th grade and found out she loved art even more. She became a good artist and wrote stories just like Joe had. They made her popular. She wrote poems and short stories and saved them to be published one day. She too made up fake radio shows and loved the real Christian radio shows. She wrote Adventures in Odyssey every week when she heard a new show. She had heard every show at least 6 times.

She loved Whit. She thought he was the coolest person ever, and she wished she could work at Whit's End because it sounded so cool.

She too did not want to move in 2009 when her family moved to South Carolina. She cried a lot. But she was mature and trusted Jesus. She had become a Christian at age 6 at a Bible conference in North Carolina. Her family attended every year until it closed in 2005 and a new conference center opened. She heard Bible verses and wanted to go to Heaven, not hell. Her dad and mom had shared the Bible stories for kids with them every day when they were kids.

She was always taught the right way. She loved the Bible conference center and now it was a public school she would always love it. The dorm rooms they had stayed in and she became a Christian in were made into classrooms. They refurnished buildings and rebuilt others and it looked nice when Michelle went back to visit and took some pictures in 2013.

Michelle loved high school in South Carolina after moving there. She never had more than 20 in her class, and graduated in a class of 12, 8 girls, 4 guys. She was best friends with Sarah and Angel and Misty. Britton, Amanda, Linde, and Ashley were the girls. The guys were Matt, Josh, Ryan, and Scott. The class behind them had 22 seniors, than 27, then 20, and then 34. Michelle liked having a smaller class and knowing everyone. Of course, she danced with every guy she graduated with. They were all very close tight friends. She wrote for the paper and took pictures for the yearbook. She made A's and B's. She was in the art club, and drew pictures for all. She graduated Friday May 24, 2013.

She loved youth group and church. She hung out with good Christian friends. She loved Putt Putt. Her youth group met at the church hut building. They got together every Sunday morning and night and Saturday nights in the new church gym. She helped in the nursery and in the little kids Sunday school sometimes. She loved her friends very much. She loved the youth director and the teachers and helpers. They had great games, activities, and lessons she loved. It was her favorite thing. In the summer, they went swimming a lot. They met at people's homes and got together. She loved to swim when it got real hot. She loved seeing snow whenever it snowed in the winter. She liked having short pony tails as well. People liked her hairstyles. She never had it too long. She could make friends easy with a sweet nice kind personality who gave others help and advice and drew pictures for people. She and Joe were alike in some areas.

Michelle was accepted to Ivy Bible College in the fall of 2013. She had been going to junior college. She heard Joe was there. She thought his story was awesome. She would tell her friends she would marry him one day and it would be a great romance story. When she heard he was coming to town and speaking, she was crazy with happiness. She met him and wrote him some. She had a crush on him. She did good at college, and started at IBC in January 2014. She was excited.

She made mostly A's and B's with some C's. She loved IBC over the next 2 ½ years, She was close with Joe and hung out with him and she was his buddy. They went on a few dates. She did get somewhat jealous of his girlfriends when he had one. She had a boyfriend named Ben for 6 weeks sophomore year, but things ended badly. She dated a guy named Mark for a month junior year, but they were just too much different. Mostly, she stayed single and had many friends.

She did her internship helping teach at a local Christian elementary school. It was not the one she had attended some. She helped in k-5. That was fall of her senior year. She also taught Sunday school at a local church and helped in the nursery and children's church. Sometimes she helped at the local housing project with Joe, and talked to the girls and helped them. 6 girls were saved in the 5 years they were here. She too was big on taking pictures and filling up albums. She loved pictures.

Michelle wanted to work with youth and children. That is why she wanted to teach 1st or 2nd grade and help at a church. She had some goals. She wanted 2-3 kids. She wanted to travel some and settle in the Southeast and have her husband teach or preach. She wanted to minister to girls and help them become Christians or grow in the faith and know God more.

Michelle told her parents and friends she hung out with Joe some and wanted to date him. She felt he was God's choice for her. It had gone beyond a girl crush and talking about stuff. She really felt he would marry her. She wrote a husband a love book since she was 13 with poems and stories and about her life. It was a diary at times. She would give it to her husband whenever they got married. She started praying for him daily at age 11. She was sure Joe was the best man out there. She did not care about the age difference. However, her parents did care a lot about their ages. They loved what Joe had become. They were cautions when they knew of his past. But they knew God had truly changed his heart and Joe was now on fire for the Lord. But they were worried their daughter who had never done much bad, had never kissed a boy, was loving a man who had kids older than her and had gone through many women in bed, 2 divorces, drugs, beer, many problems. He was tested for STDS and never had any. They loved when he preached at their church for a while. He was a polite young man who showed their daughter the ultimate respect. He showed them respect. He loved Jesus and was an excellent speaker and loved kids and was a cool person. Her parents wanted to get to know him more. He wanted to get to know them more. He had promised Michelle they would date this fall.

That fall had come. They were seniors. It was fall 2016. Joe and Michelle started dating Labor day September 6th. They were happy. They fell in love that October. They were both doing good in school. They got closer and closer. People realized they would get married one day and girls started dating other guys. Joe and Michelle were getting very serious now. They still spent time with other friends. They spent 4 days together and 3 days with others. Well, they did have dinner together every night.

Joe was now an admissions worker. He mainly just gave tours on Fridays and emailed 3 prospective students. He loved history and tours, and telling people the history of each building on campus. He had it all memorized. There were only 800 students, and it was small school everyone loved. The seminary and a Christian school were also there on campus.

He still did the campus radio show, but not the main one. He worked in the lab on Mondays only. He did the ministries and preached and taught a lot. He spent a lot of time with ministry and friends during 3 days. He only had 2 main classes, and one on Tuesday nights. He had decided to go to seminary one year and was accepted. He could get a Masters of Christian Education through classes and correspondence in 3 semesters of school. He would start in Spring 2017, even before he technically graduated from college. He would take 1 college course and 2 seminary classes and graduate with his class. He was thankful for that and was very excited. He was doing well

97

in classes. All those earlier correspondence courses had helped him a lot. He took some online that was easy but accredited. He had done 12 hours from an online Bible college he was able to add on to his prior total when he first came to the college. He was proud of himself. His family was also thankful and proud as his graduation date was getting closer. Michelle came and spent time with them over Christmas, and he spent time with her family and it was all good. They loved each other and the families loved the other.

Her family had accepted facts. They sat down and had a long talk with Joe one Saturday when they came to visit. The whole point of the visit was this talk. They talked about the 17 year age difference. They talked about his past. They talked about how much she loved him and how they had grown to love him too. He assured them with the money from his ex father in law, and the books and stuff he was set for life. A movie deal was in the works for his life story so well. People knew he would marry Michelle one day by now. They had talked about how fame would be good or bad for them. They assured him they forgave his past and was glad he was for God now. And Joe and Michelle had their blessings to get married.

Michelle and her parents talked about the arguments they had before they got to know him good. They did not want their daughter to date Joe. They told her not to date him. Some arguments were bad and ended in tears. She had to tell him no. For 5 weeks they did not talk in April 2016. It was killing them both inside seeing each other but not talking. Her parents said not to. They saw what it was doing to her. They said she could date him some, but that was when they were just friends. They started dating big time that fall and fell head over heels in love. They loved picnics, mini golf, bowling, movies, walks, watching TV, studying, reading, singing, and just hanging out together and it was all good.

There was a beautiful spot on campus. It was on a hill. It overlooked 2 lakes, some woods, a park, a golf course, 2 interstates, a meadow, some buildings, and a railroad track. It was beautiful. A waterfall was nearby. It was called the Pointe and was at the end of Faculty housing road. The president's home was there, and 2 gazebos. It was a perfect place to have picnics and study and be with friends some. There was a little stone building and a wall. You could fall in love up there with the view. Joe and Michelle and had picnics there and studied and hung out for hours up there. They looked for it on the interstates. They prayed and read the Bible. They talked of marriage and kids and goals and dreams.

In February 2017, they were set to graduate in 3 months. Joe felt it was time. He decided to propose marriage. They had gotten so close doing all the things they did. He got a nice ring at May's Jewelers in Ivy. It was a nice diamond ring. They would marry the day he graduated from seminary since everyone would be there to see that anyways. He got her 2 friends to get her up there on Valentine's Day. They went to the gazebo. A jet flew overhead that said "Michelle, will you marry me?" Joe came up from behind. Michelle started crying. They were very happy tears. Joe got down on one knee and asked her to marry him.

"Yes, yes, yes!!" she cried happily. "I will marry you!!"

He was very glad, he cried some too. They hugged a lot. They kissed each other on the cheeks and hands. They were the happiest people alive. They spent the next few hours up there. They were there at 6:11 when he proposed and 10:15 when they went back to the dorms.

They of course planned the wedding for the day Joe knew. He would graduate from seminary on Saturday May 12, 2018. They were so happy. Michelle went back to the dorm and showed the ring to everyone. Joe told all the guys he was close to. All the girls wanted to see the ring. Some were a tiny jealous, but had to come to know Joe and Michelle were the perfect couple and were so sweet and cute together. They were everyone's favorite couple on campus. Everyone loved them. All the girls hugged her and danced and they were drinking coke and cake and making wedding plans already. They ate way too much ice cream. They were a little wild. Some acted like Lauren. Soon every girl on campus knew by 11:30. By the end of lunch time the next day, everybody on campus knew and everyone saw the ring that week. It was so great for all. People who graduated this May would come back next year. It was happy times.

Joe and Michelle made all A's the rest of the year. They spent time with all the good friends. Joe helped many guys. He visited many people in a few months. It was good times. They had met many good friends. Even though they would be there one more year, most of their class was moving to new places or back home to start their lives. Out of 188 people in the class, 17 were staying in Ivy. 13 were going to grad school or work. Michelle was going to be a k-4 aide for the next school year at Grace Christian, the same school she had interned at the previous spring, and she had loved the school.

Joe and Michelle graduated May 13th. Many family and friends came for the joyous day. It was a nice weekend. He graduated with honors. She had made good grades as well. They had a big reception and party and it was good and they were happy. The speaker was good. They took a lot of pictures and promised to stay in touch with departing friends and see each other at Homecoming every year when they could and special occasions. They were glad they had made such friends.

They had a good summer. They spent time with the families. His daughter Michelle got married that June. They had a tough time at first knowing their step mom was younger than them. They had a tough time accepting her at first. They were not happy at first. They too grew to love and accept her. But not without blasting Joe at fist. They were happy for their dad. They were good women. Michelle married Frank Burns in June. Rebecca was engaged to be married to Steve Morris that January. They were both going to live in the Atlanta area and work there and live their lives and they were happy.

They both worked at Camp Faith Time. He was a counselor and helped in worship. She helped in the kitchen and helped with games. She loved it as much as he did. They did another great time. The new housing was built on the other side of the gym/cafeteria building. It was beautiful. They loved staying in the new rooms and so did everyone else there.

The next school year went by quick. Michelle loved teaching. She loved the kids. Joe made awesome grades with all A's. He worked for admissions and helped teach. He was about to finish his IBC book diary to be published. He finished at the computer lab. He finished his courses and was ready to graduate. He had made many friends here and said bye to them all.

Joe was loving grad school but he was ready to end school and get on with his life. He was offered a job in November to travel for 2 years around the USA and travel and do evangelism work. He prayed about it for a week and he and Michelle decided to accept it. They had always wanted to travel. After that, he would do church/school work and she would teach school somewhere. They wanted it to be somewhere in the South East, maybe even the Carolinas. He had been offered a job in Strawberry as real small Bible college, but had to turn it down. Traveling is what he wanted to do.

Joe signed a movie deal. It would end with the wedding and come out in February 2019 for Valentine's Day weekend. People were excited and the cast had been cast for the new movie. The publishers would publish the Ivy College book Thanksgiving week.

Joe continued to mentor people. He welcomed new freshmen and students. He was kind of a Co-RA and helped the dean of students unofficially. He had been assistant youth director at Ivy Community Church since 2016. He enjoyed that and learned even more from youth directors how to do things. He invented even more new games and taught them crazy stuff and they had lots of fun.

Joe spent time with faculty and students. He paid for people to attend. He finished up his worship and Bible studies and turned them over a mature student who was 24 named Wayne. He was divorced and now a Christian and dating a sweet girl. Joe was now ready to get married. He finished his final exams with flying colors and now was ready for a big weekend.

Chapter 11
Starting Anew

May 11 and 12, 2018 came quickly. They had the reception party early Friday night at 4 PM. It was at restaurant nearby the school ran. They had rented it out for the night. It was a nice place. The people toasted them and shared memories. There was pictures everywhere and albums and poster boards. It was looking very nice. There was a lot of family and friends. Even more would be there the next day for the real big day and Joe and Michelle loved seeing everyone and spending time talking with them. They stayed there for 2 ½ hours and had good fellowship. It was after the wedding rehearsals. Only the wedding party and some main family members were there for the rehearsal. They felt ready.

Afterward, the night was just beginning for them. They then went to school for baccalaureate ceremony. They were there for a while and some of the reception. The families loved everyone and it was good. The speaker was good. He challenged them. It was the mayor of Millbrook and the former governor of Georgia. He was a good man and been a Christian since he was a small boy of 5. His dad and both his grandparents and 2 of his uncles were all preachers.

Graduation was good. The families cheered for Joe when he walked across the stage and got his degree. It was exciting. There was posters and noise makers and yelling. It made the national news as the local media was there. It was great. Joe was one of the first 5 named called with the name Allen. Some moms with kids sat in the back at the end of the rows came in , left for a while, and came back and cheered for his name. They then left for a while again. Most stayed. The real young kids were in the nursery the whole time. The former college president who had left after their freshmen year to do mission work in Spain gave the address. He was now going to be a college chaplain at Oakley Bible College.

The media was not at the church. The rehearsal had gone good. People knew their jobs and places. Michelle was ready. This would be her only marriage. She said that. She was crying before hand. She had 6 close friends from high school and college. He had the same. He cried a little when he saw her walking down the aisle. She cried some too. He cried during the vows. They wrote the vows. There was slide shows of them growing up and people loved that. The wedding went very good and people was moved. They were married at last. Michelle's high school crush dream had come true.

" I, Joe, take you, Michelle, to be my lawfully wedded wife. I promise to make you the only woman in my life I can truly love. I have learned a lot from past failures. I have seen not as good love. I have been to hell on earth a few times. God has saved me from hell or jail. And now so have you. I love you so very much. You are my sunshine, my love. I want to wake up and see you every morning. You will be the only woman I will kiss and sleep with and be there. Thank you for waiting for me. I do not deserve you in so many ways. I promise to love you, cherish you, hold you. You will be the mother of my children .I love you more than words and deeds

103

can ever express. Jesus gave me to you, and He gave you to me. I will care for you and help you in any way I can. We will be partners in Christ together. We will go through the good and bad together. I will love you for better or for worse. You are the reason I love and want to marry again. I love you with all my heart. I will love you forever here until death do us part. I take you, Michelle."

"I, Michelle, take you, Joe, to be my lawfully wedded husband. I promise to make you the only man in my life I can truly love. I love you so very much. You are my sunshine, my love. I want to wake up and see you every morning. You will be the only man I will kiss and sleep with and be there. I have been waiting for you. I have held out for you and waited. You are the only husband for me. I love you more than words and deeds can ever express. Jesus gave me to you, and He gave you to me. I will care for you and help you in any way I can. We will be partners in Christ together. You will be the father of my children. We will go through the good and bad together. I will love you for better or for worse. You are the reason I love and want to marry again. I will love you forever here until death do us part. I take you, Joe."

The reception was nice and everyone greeted them. It was very good. They were happy. They had good toasts. A lot of family and friends were left happy and crying. Lauren gave some entertainment. Their car was rolled and was ready for them. The wedding was at Ivy Baptist Church. It was packed. The gym was packed and it was a nice time.

And then they threw stuff at them and waved goodbye. They threw the rice and the good stuff and it was good. The reception continued for a while.

They honeymooned on a cruise to the Bahamas. They were gone Sunday-Thursday and it was an awesome time. Michelle had her first kiss and waiting for marriage for sex was so worth it. They had a great time and it was wonderful. They took many pictures. They met other Christians and made new friends. They danced and ate a lot. There was good food. Lauren again gave good entertainment Joe shared his classic stories and jokes everyone loved so much. These people were hearing them for the 1st time. Joe and Michelle did get lot of privacy. But they were famous. People wanted to know if it was really them. People would turn around and stare at them. They walked into rooms and people got quiet and then they heard whispering. Joe signed a lot of papers. They ate at all times of the day. They stopped in Freeport and Nassau and got t-shirts and lots of souvenirs. They laughed at the stuff .

And they were now happily married and ready to start their new lives and ministries as traveling evangelists. They would leave in August after camp. They would spend time with the families that summer and vacation a little. They would live in his little home in Hammonds, the one behind his parent's home he had built. It was 3 bedroom, 2 bathroom with a den, living room, prayer room, and kitchen. It was not that big, and was a guest house in a lot of ways and people stayed there.

The next 3 months went by ok. They argued some. Michelle had to get used to living with a man not her dad or brother. But she was used to them at times. They argued about some stuff. Marriages always start off rough in some areas, especially if they are just now living together. They, as Christians, felt you should only get married to live together. Joe had realized it is wrong to live together, no matter how much ya'll are in love. He wished he had waited more. But you can't live in the past and with regrets. He lived for future, and for his new love and marriage and for the Lord.

Joe and Michelle were still getting used to this. They saw his family a lot. They helped start a new church in the area. She was teaching summer school at Hammonds Middle School. The students loved her and she taught English and History.

Marriage is the toughest partnership. But they were making it work. They argued but made up. They never went to bed angry at each other. They prayed and read the Bible together every day. They read good Christian commentaries. They had set up an engagement website, and now set up their wedding and marriage website. It was very popular and was signed my many. Their myspace pages were popular and had thousands of friends. They also had private ones only real close family and friends knew about. They had fun on the internet. They put on videos of Joe and Lauren as kids being their usual goofy silly crazy gross self. They were little goobers. They had videos of her as a kid, and many videos of them together at college and wedding and marriage. They thought of new stuff to do a lot. They put them online and everyone loved them. They also had videos of him speaking and preaching and stuff. They were popular sites. Sometimes as many as 10,000 came to the pages a day. They kept journals online. They planned to write a marriage book for newly married couples. They were learning a lot. He had gone through 2 failed marriages. But he had changed so much since then. They wanted kids, but after the tour was over. They had people over for dinners and fellowship. They loved watching DVDS and movies and TV together. They sang a lot in church. They released a CD as camp went on. They taught a local Christian drama team and helped out with a lot of stuff for them. People became better actors and they gave good tips. Michelle taught girls to sing better and helped in voice lessons.

Summer school ended in July. They visited in Strawberry. Everyone had met Michelle before, and loved her. They stayed with good friends. He helped preach at revival 2 nights. He went on the radio show and they interviewed Michelle and Joe. They talked about married life and Bible college and about the future evangelism work. They were there for 5 days and saw everyone he had known before. It was a fun good time. She even got to see the Mississippi River which she had not seen in years when they lived in Texas. It was an hour from Strawberry and they took pictures and a video.

They were at camp for teen week for 2 weeks. It was as awesome as always. They were counselors and helped with music and worship. Lauren and her family were there as well. The two weeks' themes were Life is a Highway and Pirate week. They were both very successful and fun. The long time directors of the camp were retiring after 36 years. They were

69 now. They would still come during the week every summer, just not direct. They got a big party and standing ovations and presents and a special ceremony and songs and it was special evening. Many people cried. It was sad at times. They loved the camp, and that is why they would visit each year. They were big at the camp and in serving the Lord.

Joe and Michelle went to see 2 Atlanta Braves games. And then they went to Walnut Grove, Minnesota and De Smet, South Dakota. They also saw Pepin, Wisconsin. These were all homes of Laura Ingalls Wilder, and they had always loved the show and books. They waded in Plum Creek and took lots of pictures. It was cool seeing where she had lived before. It was awesome. They loved the dramas the people acted out. They had a good trip. They were happy they had finally come. They had wanted to come for years. They would see other sites she had lived later on at another time.

Joe and Michelle were back in early August. They were still getting used to marriage. They were making compromises and changing some stuff to make the other one happy. They saw movies at the theater every weekend. They read books to each other. They did devotions during the breakfast and at night. They lay in bed and talked and looked to future. They had their own sides of the bathroom. They would keep a lot of stuff here when they left to travel. They bought an RV for the evangelism trips. Others would come too. They would go to all 50 states and even Canada. They had dressers in the RV for clothes. They took all Adventures in Odyssey albums ever made plus 10 hours of preaching and some sports talk radio and 40 hours of music. They took audio tapes and CDS. Plus DVD players and 2 portable TVS.

The next 2 weeks were getting things together. Joe spoke to 2 or 3 different groups a day. He spoke at churches and local organizations. They spent time at Chuck E Cheeses, their all time favorite restaurant. They spent time with friends and family. Her family spent a few days there. They sang at churches and he shared his story and his stories again. They swam a lot at the neighborhood pool. They went to local ball games and saw the Braves a few times. They sat in box seats now and had a good time. The Braves were 5-1 when they went to see them play. They would also watch the games on TV.

Joe's old friend from Carters Madison was now a lawyer. He stopped by and visited which was good for both men who had not seen each other in years. They caught up. Madison was now married with 2 young girls and a son on the way. His wife Rebecca was beautiful. They had similar beliefs, as they were Mormons. They all had a good visit as well and were happy.

Joe and Michelle watched a 4 year old girl named Heather for 4 days. She was curious about being a parent some and being in charge of a little one. They were good friends with her parents and Heather had a good time. They went to the park, swimming, the local zoo, the nearby waterfall at the Bible college, bowling, skating, and mini golfing. They watched fun Christian videos for kids. They sang at night and read her Bible stories for kids. They enjoyed her company a lot.

Joe spent a couple of Sunday nights with the church youth group. They played a game of ultimate dodge ball. They played a game where you played baseball and ran around the bases backwards. Joe did the lessons for the group.

The church had a 75th year anniversary the week before they left. Michelle made some cookies. Joe helped work on the history part of program. It was enjoyable. A lot of people came back, including 2 previous pastors. The members sang songs of past and tried in the various styles of each decade for a few nights and it was a real nice celebration. They were sorry when it was over.

Joe and Michelle spent the afternoon at the college waterfall. They had a nice romantic picnic and talk. A few people came and went. They climbed on the rocks some and had fun. The best picture had been the day it had snowed at Christmas the year before and it was beautiful. They took some pictures now and they turned out good as well. They talked of the road and all that would come with it. They loved each other and knew their love would overcome anything with God's help. All marriages have problems. But compromises and work helped. He brought her presents and she bought him little stuff. They celebrated every month on their monthly anniversary by going out to dinner. He did silly things. He would dress up and go places and give candy to kids. He would sing silly kid's songs as they walked through stores and restaurants and banks. One time he dressed up like Santa Claus at a Brave's game and made it on TV.

They cleaned the whole house Thursday before leaving. They knew guests would stay there. They had a lot of stuff in the basement. They took the clothes books food drinks CDs audio tapes with them. They had a big get together at the church that night and it was good fellowship. They gave everyone a booklet with a funny story and crazy pictures. It was only 12 pages. They took more pictures. And Joe and Michelle took off Friday morning for the new adventure of road evangelism. The family and some friends came to see them off. And they were ready to start the tour that night.

Part Three:
Ministry

Chapter 12
Traveling Speaker

Joe and Michelle hit the road for the next 2 years. They had a great experience and saw a lot of places and met a lot of people and enjoyed the various churches and schools and organizations. They went to every state and a lot of cities. They stayed in people's homes from churches that had invited them. They were always the best guests, and brought pictures and presents in a way to say thanks for the use of the home. They especially liked staying at homes with children.

Joe was 40 and Michelle 23 when they started the new ministry. They loved the time in the RV as well. With music, AIO, talking, and singing together they were never bored. They had found RA parks online to stay in, and it was always good.

They started off in South Carolina, and spoke at 6 churches in one week. They also spoke to 2 schools. They appeared in Ivy and Lansing of course with the first stop being her hometown. Joe stayed with some old friends he had known for years. One night they stayed in the college alumni building. They stayed at Michelle's parent's home as well and loved it.

Joe spoke at Ivy Christian School one Tuesday morning. He challenged the group. The older ones knew him from ball games he would attend. There were still a couple of teachers from Lansing Christian School who had been there for years and was still there. There was some students who were in class with him and had come back to teach or be the principal. They remembered each other a little bit. Michelle spoke to some women's groups there as well. 20 people were saved in South Carolina.

They spoke at 12 churches and 10 schools in North Carolina. Of course, they stayed in Carters since he used to live there. The older people from the church were still there and were glad he was good and living for Jesus. No one was left at the school from when he was there, but they had heard of him. He told the school funny stories of all the stuff he had done there and all the experiences. Chapel went over by 45 minutes, and no one minded. He got 2 standing ovations. 3 people were saved, and 10 recommitted their lives. All the students gathered around him all day to talk to him. He was in the cafeteria the rest of the day at a table near the entrance for people to come talk to him and he was very popular.

They visited Mt. Airy for a day. They enjoyed seeing Andy Griffith's hometown and all the Mayberry stuff. It was a good stay. They were not speaking there, but wanted to stop by and see the place. They stayed in Andy's old home overnight and loved that.

They visited the state capitol and the capitol building and saw the monuments. The governor gave them the key to the city. They attended a couple of minor league games and spoke at their Faith days after the game was over and a lot of the fans had left. Joe spoke at the groundbreaking of 4 new churches, 2 new schools, and a new Habitat for Humanity.

They met a nice couple at a RV park in the Florence area. They were 30 and new Christians and had been married for 3 years. They were unable to have kids due to heath reasons.

They had read some of Joe's writings and she had loved his comic strip back in the day. Bob and Jenny were looking at adoption ideas. Joe and Michelle helped them by showing ideas and praying with them about stuff. Bob and Jenny were going on a RV trip from Florida to Virginia and were enjoying their trip. They came to see Joe speak at the church and enjoyed hearing him. They promised to now stay in touch.

They had a good stop in Newton. They spoke at a FCA event and 2 churches. The church was having a mission's conference the next weekend and Joe helped set up for it the morning after he spoke. 12 people were saved at the school which was a great experience. 2 girls shared of recent pregnancy scares and said they did not want to go through that again. They asked Joe to pray for them they would be abstinent and remain pure for marriage from now on. 2 football players told him they were all big on athletics, the biggest most popular boys in school, could get any girl, but were not truly happy. They went to a Christian school, and did not truly know God. Joe helped them and prayed with them. They did not become Christians there, but promised to think about it more. 2 people told him they were atheists and were forced to come here. Joe respectfully and gently said he would pray for them. Again, he hung out in school cafeteria, as he did that a lot. He met some cool people, and helped with advice and problems and prayed with them.

They wrote emails weekly to let people know how they were doing and kept people updated on the entire ministry and what was going on.

Joe and Michelle were in North Carolina a week and a half. 57 people came to God, and 128 rededicated their lives. They spoke at a Labor Day conference, where 50 people recommitted their lives at one time. They stayed with 6 pastors and their families.

In Tennessee, they stayed for 2 weeks and spoke at a church revival in Grovetown. They spoke there for 4 nights and stayed with the youth director. It was nice. They had 2 kids and another on the way. 22 people were saved and 233 rededicated their lives. Joe's stories and jokes had people cracking up for several minutes. He later had them in tears. He attended a local middle school football game Thursday afternoon before church started. The mayor gave him the key to the city.

Joe spoke at Marshall. His friend Brian from elementary school was the pastor there and he invited him there. He and his wife Kathy had 6 kids aged 4-16. Joe stayed in the basement and some of the kids doubled up for 2 nights. He spoke at a special chapel Tuesday morning at the Christian school and stayed for lunch. He then spoke at a public school as long as he didn't get into religion too much, just avoiding drugs and drinking. He was popular with the youth. He took place in a charity basketball game that night and scored 10 points. They raised $ 3,300 that night for a cancer patient. She was 12 and needed surgery. She was able to be at the game that night. She loved Joe and had pictures with him. Laura was a strong Christian and her faith in God was even stronger now and the cancer did not cause her to doubt.

Joe spoke to various churches and schools around the state. He met the governor, 7 mayors, 10 congressmen and 4 men from senate. 82 people were saved and 367 rededicated their lives and every night was a success. They even led a couple to Christ at a RV park and promised to stay in touch. They walked into a Huddle House and people asked for autographs. They got to be extras in a movie. They went to an amusement park one day and had a blast. They went to a zoo one day as well.

They stayed 4 nights in Oakley, Virginia. Mark and Lauren used to be at church there. Michelle's dad was there, he had been there 12 years and she was born there. It was homecoming at Oakley Bible College and then the church, so Mark spoke that Sunday night. Joe spent time with the Bible college students at the soccer game. They agreed that would be a great place to work one day. They spoke at Oakley Christian school Monday morning and 3 people were saved and 6 rededicated their lives. Michelle's dad was also popular with the students since he used to be the dean. Joe and Michelle were able to see her old home. It was now the home of the head of maintenance. It was right there on campus on faculty row. Michelle and Joe were able to take a tour, 2 more bedrooms and an office had been added since she lived there. Lauren and Mark drove by their old home. It too had been added onto. An atheist family lived there now people told them. Some old neighbors were still around. Michelle's old principal from South Carolina lived in Oakley now, and had them over for dinner one night. He shared stories of how many people told him how much they respected her, her faith and decisions. He thought it amazing she had never kissed a guy before marriage. He found it somewhat ironic she had married a man with so much experience and failed marriages, but knew she was the type to forgive and accept others and love them. He said she had been much loved, and people wanted to be more like her. This humbled and surprised her, and she was shocked in some ways. She was glad she had touched so many lives.

They had some real good experiences in Virginia. 30 people were saved and 212 rededicated their lives. They spent the day with Evangelist J Morris and his family and enjoyed them. Joe and Michelle did some skits for the kids. Lauren and her kids tagged along and also did some skits and stuff. J let him speak Sunday night and share of his life and experiences.

In West Virginia, 12 people were saved and 34 people rededicated their lives. Joe spoke at a groundbreaking at chapel/fine arts building at a Christian school and later at a nursery/preschool building at a church nearby. He worked at a Habitat for Humanity restore for a day and spoke on a public radio show. He spoke at a 'Say no to Drugs' rally concert and sang with some bands.

Joe and Michelle toured Washington D.C. They saw all the main buildings and enjoyed it. They met the president and had dinner at the White House. They stopped at the capitol building and met some people they had always admired. He spoke at the steps of the Lincoln Memorial. He spoke at the National church and 9 other churches. They saw John F Kennedy's grave and the Vietnam War Memorial. They stayed at Mason's home, a friend, in Alexandria. They also stayed in Arlington one night at her cousin Cathy's home. They saw the Ford Theatre where Lincoln was shot. Joe spoke at a Promise Keeper's rally that weekend. He spoke at the grand opening of a new exhibit at the Smithsonian Museum. 80 people were saved and 140 rededicated their lives.

In Maryland, 34 people were saved and 75 rededicated their lives. They met some movie stars at various places. They saw 2 Orioles World Series games, and pulled for Atlanta. The Braves won 2 of 3 in Baltimore, and won the series in 6 games. They lost game 1-0 and trailed 6-1 in the 8th inning and exploded for 7 runs. They won 12-6 and the momentum carried them to a World Series win. Joe and Michelle were happy. They met several players from some stars. This is where they met most of the movie stars and musicians and famous people they met there. They got several autographs, and handed out many as well.

Joe spoke at Axley Bible College. They gave him an honorary degree which truly humbled him. He attended the 1st home basketball game, and spoke to the team in the locker room. They gave him a game ball afterwards, signed by the whole team.

Joe helped in the groundbreaking of a Christian coffeehouse in Mio. He spoke at a dedication of a new gym in Bakersfield. He met with the mayor of Johnson about stuff. They camped out in a church parking lot in the RV. Joe helped a pastor with a computer problem.

20 people were saved in Delaware. 63 people rededicated their lives. They stayed in the governor's mansion and loved that. They sat around with his kids and acted silly and told stories and listened to 3 Odyssey episodes. They got each email address to stay in touch.

In New Jersey, 245 people were saved and 890 rededicated their lives. They spoke at the Jet's stadium. 8000 people came for that. It was at a youth rally. They spoke at 12 colleges, 18 churches, and 8 schools. They were there until early December. They were busy almost every minute there. They helped at a YMCA one day and had a blast. They were sorry to go.

They were in Pennsylvania 2 weeks. They spoke at 11 churches and 5 schools. 100 people were saved and 333 rededicated their lives. They stayed in some great RV parks. They stayed with 3 pastors as well. They spent some nights staying in RV, and sometimes in people's homes. They wanted some of both. Lauren and her family came up one weekend and people got a kick out of them, especially little kids. Joe played in a charity basketball game and raised $ 6,000 for Habitat for Humanity house building project. They went to a Philadelphia NBA game. He met the governor at the game and got a ball autographed by the 76ers and Celtics and enjoyed it very much. He was interviewed on TV during the game. He spoke at Millwood Bible College and the Christian school. He had considered MBC, but did not want to go that far from home. He also spoke at the PCA church there, and agreed to go back every year.

They went back to Hammonds and Marshall for the rest of the year. It was almost Christmas. The movie opened up on December 20th about his life, ending at graduation. It had many positive reviews and was rated PG-13 for drugs, alcohol, and some language. It made $ 22 million opening weekend, and went on to make $ 134 million nationwide. It would turn out to be popular on DVD in the future as well. They had a good Christmas, and spent much time with family and it was good.

Naomi was 20 and a junior at Ivy Bible College and engaged to be married the December of the senior year. Mark was 18 and a freshman at Hammonds Junior College working on an associate's degree. Suzanne was 14 and a freshman at Hammonds Christian School and was on the volleyball and soccer teams and had her 1st boyfriend. The family was very happy.

Joe went to the last Atlanta Falcons game of the season and spoke at a rally afterwards. They visited Monk 2 nights and saw some old friends. They had a good Christmas and New years, and enjoyed the family fellowship. And now it was 2019.

They went to New York for a month. They spoke at 22 churches, 12 schools, and 2 rallies. They saw the Knicks play and the Giants lose the NFC championship. They went to the Freedom Tower and Empire State Building. They saw 2 movies being filmed. In one, him speaking at a rally was used in the movie. He played himself in a restaurant in one scene as well. In the other, he is walking down the street and the main character recognizes him. He was paid for this, and gave the money to a local church building a new fellowship hall. They appreciated it. He also spoke at 2 colleges and 1 seminary. 124 people were saved and 678 rededicated their lives. They met with the governor one afternoon as well.

In Massachusetts, he had a blast. He enjoyed Boston and all the places there. He even visited the "real Cheers" bar, but he did not drink any beer of course. He toured old Fenway stadium, and took in another Celtics game. He spoke in 16 churches and 10 schools. 78 people were saved and 150 rededicated their lives. He saw his old pastor, who was preaching in Hackett now.

He traveled throughout the rest of the New England states. In Vermont, 52 people were saved and 240 rededicated their lives. In New Hampshire, 82 people were saved and 35 rededicated lives. In Connecticut, it was 56 and 128. They toured ESPN and the colleges. They drove 1-95 in Maine and crossed into Canada for a while. 60 people were saved, with 120 rededications. They stayed at Camp David overnight with the President. They stayed at a mayor's home. They enjoyed New England.

They drove down to Ohio. They stopped at 22 churches and 12 schools. They spoke at 2 conferences. It was now late May, and school got out. They visited Ohio State. They visited the biggest zoo in the state. They helped build a new youth classroom at a church. They spoke at a game room/youth room at another church. 40 people were saved here, with 100 rededications.

In Kentucky, it was 222 and 763. They spoke at a dedication for a new seminary building expansion. They ate at the 1st KFC location. They spoke at 12 churches and 4 rallies around the state. In Illinois, they saw the Cubs and White Sox play and loved Chicago. They were on national Moody radio shows. They saw the Sears Tower. They spoke at Bible colleges and 34 churches. 60 people were saved and 100 rededicated their lives. In Indiana, 100 people were saved and 293 rededicated lives. They went to Michigan, and 40 people were saved and 92 rededicated lives. They were in some radio shows there as well. They got to see the Tigers play the Braves in an interleague game, and the Tigers won 11-0 on a perfect game. They were disappointed the Braves had lost like that, but were glad to see some history like that.

They were able to do some Laura Ingalls Wilder tours soon. In Wisconsin, they saw Pepin where she was born. They saw the rebuilt cabin. They stayed in Walnut Grove and saw the pageants and stuff and where she had lived on Plum Creek. They saw DeSmet in South Dakota, where she had lived and met and married Almazno. They saw the pageant here as well. They toured homes and places and saw the cemetery where most of the family was buried. They went to Burr Oak in Iowa, where she had lived for a while. They were glad to see all the places here and see the history of Laura.

They loved the states as well. In Wisconsin, 70 were saved and 120 rededicated lives. In Minnesota, it was 69 and 159. They loved seeing all the stuff here. They went to the Mall of America as well, and saw many, many lakes. They spoke at 12 churches in one week. In Iowa, it was 63 and 141. They saw the Field of Dreams and loved that. They saw the Mount Rushmore in South Dakota. There were 88 saved and 200 rededications. It was 20 and 88 in North Dakota. They enjoyed the Dakotas and the hills there. In Montana, it was 68 and 188. In Wyoming, it was 84 and 263. They enjoyed Yellowstone very much. Lauren's daughter Suzanne was 15 now and visited them for 2 weeks, including 2 nights at Yellowstone. The rest of the family came up as well to Yellowstone, including Naomi's fiancé. They had a great trip.

They counseled a week at Camp Faith Time. There was 2

people saved and 12 rededicated their lives, and they had another great experience.

In Idaho, 60 people were saved and there were 120 rededications. They drove to Seattle in late August. They stayed in Washington 3 weeks. 180 were saved here They saw Mt. St. Helens. In Oregon, they visited historic places as well. 90 were saved, and 170 rededicated their lives. Joe spoke at a new small college opening. It was to be a good little Bible college.

Word reached they needed to be back in Tennessee for little Laura's funeral. They had to have it at the gym. 3300 people came. They had a smaller family/friends memorial service at the grave. 140 students became Christians as the result of her life and testimony. 412 rededicated their lives. Everyone agreed Laura would have loved that, and she would have been glad. They were there 4 days, which would have been rest days. They did not mind. They were planning to go to Hammonds for a week, and were able to be there 2 nights. Laura's family was glad they came. She had just turned 13, but was ready to go meet Jesus. Her longtime best friend Moe kissed her last morning, so she could have kissed a guy. She loved Jesus and lived her life for Him. She helped many people and was very much loved and would be missed, but so many people came to know God because of her life. Joe and Michelle were glad they got to know her.

They spent 6 weeks in California. They saw Los Angeles, Hollywood, San Francisco, and Sacramento. He spoke at 38 churches, 47 schools and 23 colleges. 278 were saved and 1287 rededicated their lives. They loved Disneyland and other fun stuff. They met the governor. They were on 12 TV shows, and 5 movies. They met many TV and movie stars, and musicians. They filmed a video of their ministry so far and showed them speaking in California and they loved it.

They went to the other US States. They loved Hawaii and all that it was about. They went to the beaches. They spoke a lot. They saw 28 people get saved and 100 rededicate lives. They enjoyed everything. In Alaska, it was 40 and 111. They met Eskimos and saw cool things. They saw Canada border and went to Russia for a day. They stayed in an igloo. They loved it.

They got back to LA and got their RV back. It was on a pastor's farm. They went to Nevada and went by Reno and Las Vegas. 60 people were saved with 111 rededications. They spoke at a YMCA retreat, and a Promise Keeper's conference. They went tubing one day.

They saw Utah next. They saw a lot of Mormons, and camped out at Salt Lake. They saw Madison, who taught at BYU now. They enjoyed the parks.

In Arizona, they stayed in Grand Canyon again and loved it. They spoke at 24 churches and 22 schools. They spoke at 4 retreats. The numbers were 92 and 222. They loved the Phoenix area as well. They went to an amusement house and laughed a lot.

In New Mexico, it was 34 and 78. In Colorado, they loved the mountains and some ball games. They played in snow and went skiing. It was 72 and 150 here. They visited Focus on the Family and did 3 shows and were voices on the new kid's radio drama. Adventures in Odyssey had been off the air for a while, and now they had a new show that all the kids loved very much. They loved doing these shows, and meeting the Focus leaders. They were offered jobs in the ministry.

They spent Christmas with the families. Naomi married Jim Adams and she was a virgin as she married. Lauren cried. They had a good Christmas and good fellowship with families. There was some new babies. Joe spoke at 3 churches. Her family was great. One of her sisters and brothers were both pregnant. He spoke at the dedication for the new library/fine arts building at Hammonds Christian School. It was a very nice building. A family in area built on a nice back screened in porch in their Hammonds home.

In Kansas, they visited Laura Ingalls's old home. They visited the cabin and the land. They met a woman who loved the books but despised what Michael Landon had done in changing the TV show as much as he did. Michelle told her how she had always loved the Television without Pity board that made fun of Little House. The people made the most outrageous posts, and made fun of the show a lot. They showed the show was not family friendly at times. The women said she posted too, and it turned out they had talked on the board a lot, and now met in person. They were amazed. They both wanted to see all the Little House sites. They loved the cabin here, and it was a good experience for all.

60 people were saved in Kansas, and 140 rededicated lives. It was 250 and 800 in Texas. Joe and Michelle loved all the historic places. They were in Texas for 2 months and spoke at 50 churches and 30 schools. They loved the history and ranches and ball games. They saw the Rio Grande and went to Mexico for 2 days. They went to Louisiana and loved New Orleans. It was 78 and 178 here. They met more famous people, and stayed at LSU one night. They were named honorary graduates of Concord Bible College. They spoke at opening of new Christian theme park, and rode a lot of rides without standing in line. They felt like little kids again. They were given some free prizes as well.

In Missouri, they visited Mansfield where Laura Ingalls had lived for the last 63 years of her life. They saw her and Almanzo's graves. They had seen all her sites and homes. They spoke at 20 churches and 10 schools. The numbers were 70 and 155. In Arkansas, it was 80 and 178. They stopped in Mississippi and stayed in Strawberry for a week. It was 82 and 212 here. They were on the Christian radio show again. They spoke in several cities. In Alabama, it was 67 and 234. They were named honorary graduates of Jackson Bible College there. They threw out the first pitch at 3 baseball games there.

In June, after looking at ministry offers, he had accepted a job starting in September. He would be the assistant pastor and Christian Education director at Grace Community Church in Lansing, SC where his grandpa had been for 37 years. He would also teach Bible and coach junior high basketball at Lansing Christian School and he was excited about this great chance.

In Florida, he went to many places like Cape Canaveral and

124

Disney World. He spoke at many churches and schools and retreats. 189 were saved and 845 rededicated their lives. He went to a lot of historic places. He even went to Westville where Laura Ingalls had lived. He spoke at a Navy base and flew with the Blue Angels, an experience he would never soon forget. He threw out the 1st pitch at big league games and Lauren sang the national anthem. She loved doing that.

In Georgia, he wrapped up the tour in his home state. 156 were saved and 560 rededications. He got much stuff from the governor and several mayors. He had done well on his tour. He went to farms and cities and towns. He went to Six Flags and spoke at a stage. He took place in Faith Day at the Braves's game. He donated $ 300,000 to remodel and refurnish the Christian school in Monk. It would take around a year. He spoke at his old church. His old home was for sale. He and Lucy had lived there, and he had some roommates later. It was empty, and they stayed there 6 nights for $ 700. His married daughters lived in Augusta now. They were 25. His daughter Michelle and 2 year old twin sons. Rebecca had a 6 month old daughter. He loved spending time with them. He spoke at the new library dedication in Hodges, and it was a beautiful building for a smaller town. His son Luke was 15 and visited him there some. Lucy still despised him. He had also seen Luke in Texas, and she refused to see Joe. Joe loved his trip and time in Monk.

Now that was it 2020, and the tour was wrapping up, they started talking about having kids. They tried a little. They prayed God would give them kids in His own timing. They wanted 3 kids just like Lauren. Since he was his 40's they wanted to try some. Of course, she was still in her mid 20's and had more time. They talked about having kids more often now.

Joe challenged the kids at a Monk Christian camp. There was a lot of craziness in the area. There were 5 Christian schools in the area, and Monk was the largest by 50 students. 40 students had been expelled for drugs and alcohol and some witchcraft and cussing the year before. Some people said maybe 50 % of the high schoolers were Christians. There was a lot of drug abuse and pregnancies among teenagers. Some were being arrested. A lot of shoplifting, and streaking was going on. Youth group and church attendance was way low. Young Life in the area was very struggling.

They planned a 3 day event. Joe and 3 speakers were teaching. 4 athletes would be there, as well as 3 movie stars. 25,000 tickets had been sold for the events. Joe and Michelle spent hours in prayer and Bible reading and fasting. They prayed God would touch the lives of many and be at the revival and help many people repent to God and change their lives for good.

Joe challenged the youth. He compared his days under drugs to a living hell. He shared letters from 12 prisoners about life in prison. He had to stop and compose himself as he wept openly about the letters. It was heartbreaking. Many people wept at the letters, even tough football players. It shows how terrible and sad and lonely and bad prison really is. He showed them how they never wanted to go there. It talked about sexual abuse, beatings, murder and what the worst criminals would do to others. People got sick at times. He talked about the worst criminals and all they had done to get to prison, and what they did to people there. He told them to please never go to jail, and to avoid it at all costs because they did not want that.

Joe shared stories of his drugs and drinking. He told how terrible it can be and does not solve your problems. It is not the answer to anything. He told about all the deaths and sickness because of this, and all the people who went to jail because of it.

He told the story of Joseph. He had gone to high school with Joe. He was a good Christian guy and wanted to be a missionary. He wanted to serve God in his whole life. He had "the perfect" Christian girlfriend Cindy. One day in college he wanted to live a little wild. He picked up the school "easy girl" and they got drunk and high. He drove the car, and they wrecked with his girlfriend and her mom. They had been driving safely, but Joseph, the girl, and Cindy's mom were all killed. Cindy was paralyzed from waist down, and her left arm was severely injured and it took 3 years and 7 surgeries to heal properly. One bad choice had ended 3 lives, including his own, and ruined a special girl's life and her families. Cindy, however, was now a missionary to Spain, where Joseph had wanted to go and led a great ministry and was on fire for God. But Joseph's bright young future was cut short, and his bad decisions had cost many.

Joe challenged the people to change back to God. They loved Joe and his stories and jokes. They cried a lot as well. They loved the stars and athletes and music. They were taught well. 138 people were saved. 787 rededicated their lives. Many lives were touched. Many people repented of sins. Many came and talked to Joe and others. There were 600 people as counselors. Many people helped. Joe talked to many people. It was a huge success and worked well. People were glad it had such a good outcome and touched so many lives for God.

Joe and Michelle spent 2 weeks at Camp Faith Time. It was a great time as always. They did counseling and worship. 5 were saved and 12 rededicated lives. Joe and Michelle had a great road ministry and saw America. And now they were ready for ministry and staying in Lansing.

Chapter 13
Lansing

Joe and Michelle started at Lansing in mid August 2020. They were excited about what God was going to do here. His grandpa had spent 37 years at this church. He was very loved. Joe had spent years here as a regular attender and visitor. He loved the church and was so excited about being here. The old house was back in the family, his uncle lived here now. His son would live there one day and inherit it. Joe lived down the street in a 2 bedroom house. He and Michelle did not need too much. They settled in soon and some family came and helped them move in and stayed a night. And with some family right there, they knew it was all going to be good. Some church members and neighbors brought food over.

That Sunday, Joe had begun his job at the church. He was going to be the Christian Education pastor. There was a main pastor, and 2 assistant pastors were there as well. There was also a youth director and children's director. Plus they had assistants to help out. There was 600 members and 620 attended regularly. They had built a new sanctuary when his grandpa was there. In the 37 years he was there, membership went from 111 to 512. The youth group had 90-100 regulars, and the children around 160. It was good.

Joe also was going to work at Lansing Christian School. He taught freshmen Bible and coached junior high basketball. He spent 4 days Monday-Thursday at the church office after 12. He was at the school from 9-11 and then had lunch. He had practice 6-7:30 in the little gym, and 7-8 in the mornings in basketball season. The school had 2 gyms. Joe's classroom was shared with the high school Bible teacher and was right next to the main office. He had 24 students in his class, and 12 players on the team. There were 800 students at LCS. There were 8 games in the regular season, plus a tournament afterward for the championship.

Michelle took a job as a hostess/waitress at a local restaurant called Green Beans. It was a family owned restaurant and was very popular in the community. It had good home cooked food. A lot of families were regulars here. The staff was friendly. The owner and his wife were Christians and put Bible verses on the menu and in the van. Everyone was mostly nice and Michelle liked the people there a lot. She quickly became popular and worked hard and was very friendly and sweet and people requested her as a waitress. She was dependable.

Joe started that Sunday at a little special ceremony. The other church workers and elders anointed him. They had a reception after the morning church service and welcomed them. The church had some very good people and were thankful Joe and Michelle had come back to Lansing and were there to minister. Joe and Michelle met some good people that day. Their families were there as well, and they were glad.

Joe worked very good. He worked with the youth and children's departments a lot since he was the Christian Education director. Some called him like the Sunday school superintendent. He helped the teachers and looked at curriculums to use. He helped them doing programs. He helped do drama and skits and helped in talent shows. He preached at least 6 times a year. He helped talk to people who came by the church to talk and occasionally helped visit people as well. He was in charge at times when others were out. He loved this job.

Joe loved the Bible class he taught. The students were good kids. He had no real problems. They liked him a lot. He made the class fun and shared stories and stuff. No one was ever bored. He turned the Bible trivia into fun games. People thought he was a lot of fun. He let the students do skits to act the stories out. His tests were fun, hard, but not too hard. His papers were easy to figure out what to do. He had a good time. In the 8 years, people in lower grades were excited to be freshmen so they could have him. He came in a little early and stayed later to talk to people. He counseled people and prayed. He was a popular teacher. He won some awards. He spoke in chapel some. He helped sub some on Fridays.

The first year of basketball was good. They started off 1-2 and finished the regular season 6-2. All 12 boys played every game and each averaged at least 2.5 points per game. They averaged 47 points per game as a team. They won the first 2 tournament games by over 15 points. They got to the semifinal but lost 42-38. The other team was going to the championship and won. They were disappointed, but were happy with a 8-3 season. They had come off a 1-8 season, and in the previous 4 years had won 9 games, so they had done much better. The returning players were excited about the next season and the promise of a better season. They had a lot of fun, and learned a lot, and had a lot of bonding. They had movie nights with drinks, pizza, popcorn. They had parties and sleep overs. They had Bible studies and prayers and learned of God in new ways. They learned to play better. They all loved "Coach Joe."

Joe and Michelle started really to talk about having a kid in May 2021. They tried for a couple of months. In late August, it was confirmed she was over a month pregnant and was due in April. The couple was thrilled beyond words. In late September, they told the family and announced it in church.

People were excited for them. They were going to find out the gender later that year. They praised God for this new blessing.

Church was going well. They switched over to Awana for the church program for Sunday nights that September when school started back. It was a popular move. Joe preached some and worked closely with the youth department. Some of them attended the school, and the rest grew to love him as well. Of course, he shared his testimony. He hosted some talent show nights. Lauren even came to one. People laughed and when she sang a beautiful song they were very touched. Some even went to Camp Faith Time with them for 1 or 2 weeks, and loved it as well. Joe and Michelle would take young people every year.

The school year was good. The team went 6-2 and went to the championship game. They fell 50-32 but played hard all year. They finished 9-3, and were 17-6 in 2 seasons. Joe took them to 3 Braves game the opening weekend, and paid all the costs. It was an awesome trip, and the Braves were 6-0. They had a blast. They also had a lot of fun in the season at sleep overs, going to movie theaters, watching movies at homes and school, and a few parties. They were all close friends and all played and scored. They helped and encouraged each other and no one was selfish and they all grew closer to God. Joe was great at devotions.

The classes were good as well. The students were even better that his first class had been. They made class fun. He taught them a lot. He made the Bible come alive for them. Everyone participated. People wanted to memorize Bible verses. The students tried to see who could raise their hands the fastest. He helped other classes as well. He helped in chapel some. He sought students out and asked how they were. He had lunch at 11-12 in the school cafeteria with them. He came to the ball games and cheered very hard for them. He was much loved.

Adam Allen was born in April 2022. Michelle went into labor in the middle of the night Sunday night. Joe took her to the local hospital, and Adam was born at 6:13 AM. They were very happy about the new blessing God gave them. They had found out he would be a boy in December, and had many presents at the home in the nursery. It was right next to their room. They brought him home Tuesday afternoon. He had some visitors, and was very popular when he made a church appearance the 1st Sunday in May.

School ended and the summer started. They helped at church a lot. He took the team to a basketball camp in early July. He then spent 2 weeks at Camp Faith Time. Michelle came up at the end of the 1st week and stayed until the end of camp. Little Adam came up for the weekends, and was at Joe's mom's house the rest of the time. He was very popular with the campers, and was held by many. Camp was a huge success as always again. 10 were saved and 32 rededicated their lives as the workers praised Jesus for a long time.

Joe's month vacation ended with 4 days with his family and 3 days with Michelle's. They saw everyone. Joe became a grandfather as well. Michelle and Rebecca had kids the same age as their stepbrother. Luke was 18 and a freshman at Ivy Bible College, much to the anger of his mom. She said "Go, but don't ever come back here again." She disowned him and never wanted to see him again either. He would later call a few times, and even went to her house once. She hung up the phone, and slammed the door in his face. He was heartbroken, but moved on in his life. They never saw each other again. He prayed for her. He was excited to go to college and moved there in August and was close to Joe and Michelle.

The 2022-2023 school year went quickly. The team was 8-0 and was a huge success. They averaged 43 points a game, and their opponents averaged 26. They won the first game 40-22, and the second 56-18. In the semifinal, they trailed 40-30 going to the 4th quarter. The 8th graders had been with him for 3 years, and this was their last chance. They hit 4 3 pointers and outscored their opponent 21-5 and won 51-45. They rolled to the championship 51-38 and were 12-0 undefeated champions. They had gone out as winners. They had a big victory party and awards banquet, and there was much success.

Joe and Michelle threw a one year birthday party for

Adam. He had a Mickey Mouse cake. Some kids came. Some adults and youth came. It was fun. There were presents. Luke did not know all that was going on of course. He was crawling some for a while. He had taken a couple of steps as well. He was babbling a lot.

Joe was the teacher of the year at the school. He got a major standing ovation, and was very humbled. He did not want all the attention. He was spending more time at the school from 7 am until 12:30. He also coached at nights. He came to most of the home ball games. He had lunch in the cafeteria every day. He always enjoyed talking to the people then.

He was at the church from 1-5 Monday through Thursday. He helped the teachers. He subbed at times. He helped Michelle in the nursery once a month. He helped in worship and the choir. When the pastor retired in January 2023, he helped find new candidates. He preached every other Sunday and helped Wednesday night prayer services. In June, the new pastor arrived. Everyone was glad. He had been a youth director there before, and had spent time as missionary to Korea. His name was Eugene Scott, and was commissioned in late June. The church was very excited about the new pastor.

Michelle went back to Green Beans 2 nights a week in Fall 2022. She was missed a lot. Joe's cousin Ruthie watched Adam. She had a husband named Mark and were beginning to think about having kids as well. They were both 29 and been married 2 years. They were Christians and had both waited for marriage. They were in love, and worked at a real estate office and loved that.

Summer 2023 was good. Camps and church were good. Joe was gone for a month except for Sundays he was at church 3 of the 4 weeks. They spent time with families again. It was great. They had a big picnic. The basketball camp was the best yet.

The 2023-2024 school year was good. The team was 10-2 and repeated as champions, winning the last 7 games. Jack Morris was a 6th grader, and averaged 3 points and 8 assists a game. He was already a leader, and popular with many. Joe helped him a lot, and was ready for his 8th grade year. Joe helped a lot of students. He was like a chaplain in some ways. Many asked him for advice and he helped many. He prayed with many. His comics in the paper were hilarious, and very loved. He wrote a popular column once a month. Students would pose with him for the craziest photos. He had spent 4 years here.

In September 2024, he was starting his 5th school year. He was now the Junior High Sunday school teacher as well. He preached 1 Sunday a month. He was loved. Michelle told him she was pregnant September 30th. They had much to praise God about. Everyone was very glad for them. They found out it was a girl and was due that June and they were ready. Joe had 3 grandkids as well he enjoyed seeing and spending time with. Luke came 2 weekends a month from IBC.

Katie was born June 7, 2025. Adam was 3. He loved his sister, but missed being the center of attention. Michelle had quit in March and would never work at the restaurant again. She loved the job there, and was popular. But they felt it was better to spend time with her kids and raise them herself. They still ate there a lot the next 3 years. She was thankful for 5 years there. She loved it there, but had moved on to care of her kids. She loved her kids so very much and was very thankful God had blessed them twice. They planned to have more kid one day, but in a few years Lord willing.

In 2025, the team went 8-3 and lost in the semifinal. Jack missed 2 games, both losses. In 9 games, he averaged 6 points and 5 assists. The team was disappointed they did not win. But they had won 2 straight championships, and things were looking good.

In 2026, they won the championship at 11-1. Jack missed a game, and they lost that one. He averaged 8 points and 5 assists. He would go on to win JV MVP the next year, and star in varsity for 3 years. He scored 2100 points and won 2 championships. He plated for North Carolina Tar Heels for 4 years. He averaged 17 points and 8 assists per game. His senior year he was Final 4 MVP and they won their 2nd straight championship. He led them to the final 4 as a freshman. He was 8-3 against Duke. He played 6 years in the NBA, but had some injuries and never did too much averaging 6 points and 7 assists. He was rich and came back and coached junior high basketball and was athletic director at LCS for 30 years. His teams won 12 championships and finished twice 4 times. He was very popular as well, and learned a lot from Joe.

But back to 2026. They had two more years under Joe. In 2027, they went 9-2 lost the semifinal. In 2028, they went 10-2 and won the 4th championship in 6 years. Joe had won 4 championships in 8 years. His overall record was 79-14, including 4-1 for the championships.

The school years went good teaching. He helped many students. He was still great at advice. He helped many at church. He helped the Christian Education department in big ways. He was not looking to move. In April 2028, Oakley Bible College offered him the job as dean of men. Her dad had been there for 12 years. Mark and Lauren had lived up there. It was a great town. Joe and Michelle had spoken there and they decided they would like to go there one day. They prayed a lot. They sought guidance. They did not want to move Lansing. But in some ways, they felt they had done all they could do there. Joe was looking toward to working as dean of men. Church work was challenging. He felt like his dad, he wanted a new challenge. Coaching was great, but drained him at times. He wanted to get off by 5, and spend more time with his wife. He had already told the school this was going to be his last year coaching for a while, and he needed some time off. They understood. He approached the administrators in mid April and they all prayed together and read the Bible for 2 hours about what God wanted him to do and what he should decide.

Joe talked to the retired pastor, Mike Jackson. Mike told him he must go. Joe loved a new challenge. He loved people. He had loved Bible College at Ivy Bible College a lot. He loved the Christian college atmosphere. Joe had decided he would love to work at a Bible college. He thought working at one would be a dream job, maybe the best job ever.

"You must go," Mike said. "You will never forgive

yourself if you don't. I know you love it here. I know you love it here a LOT. You have made many good friends here. You have done so much good. You are a great coach, but I know you need a break from coaching. I know and respect that. I don't really want to lose you here. I know you don't really want to move. I know in other ways you are looking for new challenges. You will be good no matter where you go and no matter what you do. One day you will regret if you do not go. This is your dream job. You will look back one day and wish you had gone. It will be a regret of yours for a long time. One day, you will wish you had gone and led the ministry there. You have so much to give to men and to help them. You will be awesome and I want you to go.

Michelle and Joe were all ready to accept the job when 2 more job offers came. The church in Strawberry offered him associate pastor, 2nd only to the pastor. He would preach some and help teach. He was also offered the job teaching Bible and the athletic director at Marshall Christian School. That is where Michelle had gone to high school and her family lived there. This would also be a great job. They prayed about these jobs. They looked at options. They asked others to pray for them as well. And finally, they decided to take the job at Oakley Bible College on April 30th and told them the news.

In May, they announced to school and church they were going there. They took a Sunday off and went to visit her family. Pastor Scott announced to the congregation Joe would be leaving at the end of June. The principal announced it in chapel that Monday. Joe was gone and came back that night. Joe and Michelle had decided to miss when it was announced.

People cried a lot. They told them they would miss them a lot. They had a party. They had a lot of presents. They spent time with a lot of people. The people there meant a lot to them. They would miss a lot of people in Lansing. They were thankful God had let them serve there for 8 years.

They had grown a lot in many ways. Lots of people came up and thanked them for the years of service and all the help they had given them. They told them they were going to miss them a lot. They shared memories of the past. Joe felt he had done a lot of good for them. He felt honored he had helped many people. They were touched so many people thanked them and showed them love. They felt good they had touched so many lives. They continued to work hard and to help many people over the next month. They loved Lansing.

Joe won his 2nd teacher of the year award. The school presented him with a # 8 jersey to honor him for 8 great years. They helped hem pack. The school and church presented him with big photo albums full of good photos and good memories. There were 2 receptions. There was a big party.

Joe spoke at the church the last Sunday night in July. He preached his last sermon. It was an excellent sermon. The reception was that afternoon when they honored him and there were songs and presents. He told them how excited he was to go to a college. But he was thankful for 8 years there.

"I love you all. Thank you for blessing me and my family. We love it here. Thank you for 8 wonderful years. Thank you for all ya'll have done for us. Ya'll have helped us in so many ways. My grandpa was here so many years. I loved this place as a boy. I even lived here for 2 years. Now, I too was able to minister here. I too was able to work at an awesome church with great people. Ya'll have shown much love and grace to my family. Thank you from the bottom of our hearts. Our kids were born here. We will treasure it in our hearts for the rest of our lives. May God bless you all in the future."

Joe had made a similar speech at the school. They went to camp for 2 weeks. Adam was 5 and Katie was 3. Luke was married and had a kid on the way. His two oldest were married and had 2 kids each. The families were good. The house was sold and they would live in the dean of men's house on campus. And Joe and Michelle left in late July after camp for the next step in their lives.

Chapter 14
Oakley

Joe and Michelle moved to Oakley in late July 2028. He was now 50 and she was 33. Adam was 5 and Katie was 3. They would live here for 10 years. They were thinking of having a 3rd and final kid, but if God blessed them with only 2, they would be very content. His other 3 kids were grown and married and gave him 6 grandchildren, 2 apiece. They kept in touch and saw each other some. It was a good relationship.

The faculty members lived on campus on faculty row. The homes were set up in order of jobs and the dean of men always lived in the same house between the dean of students and the dean of women. Across the street was the dean of college/Assistant provost. They liked being right there on campus and his office was in the student center. Also on the hallway was the dean of women, residence life, married students, Student Government office, Men and Women's other RA offices, and the college chaplain. It was above the student center/cafeteria building. It was a good setup right in the middle of campus. The building was 8 years old. It was near the administration building. The old student center/cafeteria had been remodeled and converted to a small auditorium and chapel building with a small student lounge.

Joe quickly got to know the other faculty and administrators. He was already popular with them with his testimony and ministry and how he had spoken there before. He fit right in and became very close in no time. The students arrived in August and they all got to love Joe. He called all the men to his office his first month and got to know them. There were 3 dorms and 300 men on campus. There was 8 RA's and floor leaders he got to know. They got to dinner sometimes to talk and the RA's took turns being in charge at nights and on the weekends. He got to like the guys a lot.

Michelle helped him in the office on Mondays and Wednesdays. A girl named Nancy watched the kids. Joe set up his office to look very nice. He also had an office at the home. He invited students to visit him at the office and home, but not too late. He taught a class in Acts, but otherwise was in the office a lot. He sat with students some in chapel, but mostly other faculty. He sat with students in the cafeteria and fascinated them with his stories. He was well loved here too.

He was good at remembering faces and names, and he always was. He continued his tradition of encouragement notes, asking people how they were, seeking out people to say hi, cheering up the sad, and being a good friend to as many as possible. He especially sought out his guys, the leaders he had in the dorms. He needed to check on them and what was going on in the dorms. He helped students in school work. He played basketball with the guys twice a week and ran a lot and lifted weights to keep in shape. Some guys quickly joined with him and they all bonded.

He stayed at Oakley Bible College for 5 years. He was popular here and helped many guys. He got to know guys early and helped them become RA's in the future. He trained them in his way. He led Bible studies in the dorms for men. He helped start a new worship program for all on Wednesday nights. He spoke in chapel twice a year. He taught Acts all 5 years. He loved the students and they loved him. He led men's chapels twice a month. He hosted parties for kids 3 times a month and got to know the freshmen/ new students. He counseled many men in his office. He punished the rule breakers, but talked to them and prayed with them. They appreciated this and loved him. They knew they had broken the rules, and this was his job. He always gave the RA's presents as they graduated and moved on. He disciplined several guys. He made Acts come alive for so many people just like he had done in Bible. He illustrated each person and went into good detail. He made it sound like each person was right there and you could hang out with them after class. The class closed their eyes and imagined along and felt they were really there.

He hung out with them at the talent shows, coffee houses, playing pool, seeing movies at theater, and movie nights on campus. He was one of the guys at times. He also gave them space, he didn't want to smother them, and he was a faculty member. He was a rule enforcer. But he was a lot of fun in a lot of ways. People looked up to him and he helped them a lot. He enjoyed it. He was like a student in some ways. He sometimes felt he was doing too much and could be strict at times.

Joe became Christian Education director/assistant pastor at Oakley Baptist Church in 2030. He had been there for 2 years and went to church there. He was not in the office too much with college duties. He only preached less than 10 times a year. He helped the church a lot though in classes and lessons. He did some things as he had done in Lansing. He trusted the teachers and let them decide some stuff. He helped in the youth department at times and was close with Pastor Dave Brooke. They prayed together daily and had some Bible studies and stuff and it was all good.

Joe enjoyed his time at Oakley Bible College very much. He had described a Bible college job as his dream job. He loved Oakley. But in April 2033, he decided to leave Oakley

Bible College and teach at a high school and coach again. He started looking around, when the high school principal at Oakley Christian School left for a headmaster job in Ohio. He also heard the JV basketball coach was too busy at his job and could not coach anymore. Joe applied for both jobs. He also applied at Grace Christian School as Middle school PE teacher and at 3 schools in the state. He also applied at the YMCA and Civic center to coach. Then, Oakley Christian called him to interview. The junior high coach had been moved up to JV and assistant to varsity. Joe interviewed to be high school principal and junior high coach. The interview went well and seemed promising and they had him on their list of 5. He told the college he had interviewed. 2 days later, he notified them he was resigning June 30th no matter what job he ended up with. He was still at the church as well.

Five people turned Oakley Christian down. Joe accepted April 30th and would start July 7, 2033. He was very excited to be back at school and coaching. The time off had done him good. The last 4 years, they had won 30 games and were 1-1 in the championship game. They had 11 players scheduled for that winter, and they looked promising. Coach Butler would help him some as he had coached the last 5 seasons. He finished up very strong. The 4th of July the family gathered around as always in Hammonds. Joe was now 55 and Michelle 38. Adam was 11 and Katie 8. They still talked of more kids. His daughters were 39 and Luke was 29. Each had 2 kids, and would have no others. Joe had written 2 more books since coming to Oakley. His dad was near death at times, and was doing ok now. His mom was healthy for her age. Lauren's kids were grown as well. Naomi had a kid she was teaching just like her mom had taught her. She was 2 ½. Lauren had helped corrupt Joe's kids as well. Well, he helped some. It was all in good fun. They had a good family time. It was family reunion time, and more people came than usual, and they had a great time.

Jack Allen died July 21. The funeral was attended by a lot of people. Joe was down for a while. But he knew his dad was in Heaven with Jesus pain free. He had lived a good life and now was seeing his rewards. Some Bible verses and good memories, and God helped him have peace. He was close with his dad. The family took care of Joey and made sure she was ok. She stayed at the home, and the family was there. She was comforted by the fact he was in Heaven as well. He was 88 and had been married 61 years.

Joe worked hard at camp right before his dad's death. He brought 8 kids down with him. He, Michelle, Luke, Lauren, Mark, and cousin Michael all counseled. They helped in games and worship as well. The new employee lounge was very nice. It was connected to nurse's cabin and the arts and crafts room. 4 people were saved and 18 rededicated their lives.

Joe started at Oakley Christian for real August 1. He helped at church for 2 weeks when the pastor went on a mission's trip to the Bahamas. He was in the church office a lot those 2 weeks. He helped the people when they came by or called and he preached all the sermons as well. He decided to return to the pastorship one day as well, as the main pastor.

Joe enjoyed coaching the next 3 years. The first year they were 8-3 and lost in the semifinal. A 6th grader named Billy came up and averaged 2 points and 3 rebounds a game. He showed even more the next season when they went 10-2 and won the championship. He averaged 8 points and 7 rebounds a game. In 2036, he averaged 12 points and 10 rebounds a game and they were 12-0 and champs again. Just like in Lansing, they bonded and became good friends. They had the parties and sleep overs and helped each other and no one was selfish. They helped each other. They had a lot of fun hanging out. They loved the fact he coached a NBA player. They bonded and Joe helped. He coached for 3 years. Adam loved playing for his dad and played good.

Speaking of the NBA, Billy would make it as well. He averaged 26 points for the varsity team in 4 years. He finished with 3,033 points. In college, he went to Georgia. He averaged 33 points his last season and 20 points for his career. He played 16 years in the NBA and scored 30,000 points and averaged 20 points per game. He was a hall-of-famer and became very popular.

But back to 2033. Joe was a good principal for 3 years. He loved making decisions and helping the teachers. He helped the students and loved doing it. He was voted principal of the year for Virginia Christian schools in 2034-2035, and was humbled.

In December, they announced Michelle's pregnancy. People were excited. Megan was born July 4, 2034. Joe was 56 and Michelle 39. Her step-nieces and nephews were a few years older than her. She was the long awaited third child and she was quickly loved by all.

After 3 years at the school, Joe left the school and spent more time at the church. His duties increased and he was there 5 days a week. The pastor was taking a vacation from August to October to rest. Joe and the other assistant pastor were in charge a lot. They had a new youth director and children's director that helped. And soon the pastor was back and doing well.

Joe spent 2 years here like this. The assistant pastor left in March 2037 to pastor a church in Florida. Joe was second to the pastor. He did more home visits and counseled people at the church. He preached more as well. He spoke at least once a month. He spoke at various places 3 or 4 times a month. He updated his auto biography with new chapters. He was a popular speaker. He still spoke at the Christian school and attended ball games, especially to see Billy play.

Adam was also doing well on JV. He was a freshman and averaged 4 points and 3 assists per game. He had enjoyed his dad's coaching. He was close friends with all the players. He was going out with his first real girlfriend, Catherine. She was the first girl she ever kissed and he "loved" her. Katie was in junior high and was like a little Lauren. Michelle was not always thrilled with that. She was gorgeous and she could sing well. But she had blonde hair, while Lauren had black hair. She hung out with the guys and could out gross them. She ate bugs as a kid until she was made to stop. She could also be very sweet, nice, cool, polite, great manners, great class. She was the most popular sixth grader. Even the older boys were in love with her. She could not really date until high school. She had many friends and played basketball and soccer. She was a leader. She had a great laugh. She sung great, even better than Lauren. She won awards at talent shows and for her art projects. She loved science a lot as well. She was an excellent student and made great grades.

Joe led a spiritual revival in the Oakley/ Harlem/ Nathan areas. There was a lot of Christians, but a lot of other stuff going on. This was in October 2037 when school was out Monday. Gangs were causing trouble and causing some riots and messing up other people's yards. A lot of kids were having sex. Even the Christian school kids were messing up a lot. It reminded Joe of problems in Monk. It went on for 4 days. They had musicians and games and preaching. Joe shared some interesting stories. There was great food and drinks. People enjoyed themselves. Many people spoke.

Joe preached a lot. He told them they could bounce back and come back to God. He spoke of injuries he had suffered in his life." When I was 5, I was hit by a tool box and I needed stitches. When I was almost 10, I was hit by a medal swing and needed stitches. My friend Brian could not believe I was not crying. I once fell out of a tree house and hit my head but was not hurt. One time I got hit by a ball and got a black eye. One time I bumped my head at Wal Mart. One time at camp I was catching and got hit by a foul ball. I had a black eye. I caught the last 4 innings and 6 innings later that day. I was ok. I was hurt each time and bounced back. I am still good. I got over each injury. I have some scars, but that is all. It helps me remember. I am doing better now, and it was like I was never hurt. I came back better and stronger, bouncing back."

"You too can bounce back. Y'all have fallen back. Y'all have suffered injuries. You are not right with God in so many ways. Some of y'all are Christians who have slipped back. Some of ya'll have never been saved at all. Bounce back to Jesus and He will take you and make you His children. You will be better and stronger. The scars will be there to remind

144

you not to go back and sin hurts. But Jesus forgives and forgets when we repent, and wipes scars away."

Joe warned them not to be like him in a lot of ways. "Don't get involved with drugs and alcohol and sex. I did, and it ruined my life in so many ways. It will hurt you, not help you. If you have been involved, stop. Come back to God. He will forgive you. If God can forgive a terrible sinner like me, He will forgive anyone. Don't ruin your futures. They are so bright. Trashing property and being in riots can bring jail and problems and it will ruin your future. Please don't do it."

The revival was a huge success. 50 people were saved and 186 rededicated their lives. The problems were less. A lot of teens still did drugs and had sex and did some bad things. Some still cussed a lot. But police and people made sure rioting and damaging property stopped. The cities returned to normal and things were going pretty good again and all were glad.

Joe continued working at the church until summer 2038.At the age of 60, he made one more move and accepted the job as pastor of the church in Hammonds. Now it was his turn as his junior son did not want to move. Katie was not happy at 1st. But they were happy to be with the family. They had a big reception for the 8 years at the church. A new assistant pastor had started. They spent time with many friends and had good times. They had presents. They loved Oakley and spent good years there. And now they were moving on.

Chapter 15
Back to Hammonds

Joe and Michelle and the family arrived back in Hammonds at the beginning of July 2038. They had added 2 bedrooms, a recreation room, and library to the house. They also screened in the front porch. They added a bathroom in the attic. All this had happened in the last year. They knew they would live there again one day. Lauren and her husband now lived in their parents old home. They had added a bathroom, recreation room, guest bedroom and screened in the back porch and enlarged the kitchen. This is for families and grandkids. All 3 kids would live in Georgia, but not in the Hammonds area, but close. Joe's kids were also close. And his kids with Michelle were all in school and living at home.

Adam was not happy to move at first since he would be a junior. Joe felt like his dad, but Adam quickly adjusted. So did Katie, who would be an 8th grader. Her beauty, charm, humor, class, special talents, being of the guys in a lot of ways made her popular in a hurry. Megan would start preschool in the fall. She was so excited to be able to go to school and talked about it a lot.

Joe had begun preaching in mid July. They had a service and reception. Other pastors in the area spoke. Mark was 66 and had been the pastor of the church for over 30 years. He had retired, and now was just another member and attender. He anointed Joe with the other elders as he started. People said nice things, and the reception was very nice as well and many came.

Joe settled in very quickly. He preached every Sunday. He had one associate pastor, a youth pastor, children's director, music director, and 2 secretaries. There were 528 members of the church. It had doubled in size under Mark and had 4 building projects. The 1050 seat sanctuary was 2 years old. Mark had been a real blessing in his time there, and was much loved. He had many good friends and people still came to him for counseling and prayer and Bible study. Mark wrote 2 books on Bible and they were popular. Lauren was helping young ladies as well and enjoyed that a lot.

Joe was well loved in Hammonds from his life and family. He preached there 10 years, and lived there for the rest of his life. He wrote a best selling book about God's will in a pastor's decision to move to a new church. It was # 1 on the Christian sellers list for 4 months. He published a book of his life in 2037 that also became a best seller. He could retire, as he was set for life money wise. But he kept working and preaching and serving God so he would not get bored. He liked to work and stay active. He felt he would be lazy retiring "so young." He was still a very good speaker and did awesome.

Adam did well in his last 2 years of high school. He played basketball and they won the state title each year going 60-2. He averaged 4 points and 6 assists as a junior, and 8 points and 5 assists as a senior. He was far from the best but did hard and always gave his best and gave it his all. He was valedictorian and runner up for homecoming king. He was very popular and was like his dad. He helped others for school, wrote little notes, led Bible studies, sought people out, and sought people out to help. He also played baseball, and played ok. He had a couple of girlfriends and they were cool.

He attended Oakley Bible College where a lot of his friends had gone and lived on the same hall all 4 years. He graduated with honors. Again, he was like his dad and led worship in guitar, and Bible studies. He made many good friends. He dated a couple of girls, but did not meet his future wife. He graduated in 2044, and went on a 2 year mission's trip to France.

From 2046-2048 he came back and worked at a school in Marshall, South Carolina where his mom was from. He taught drama and helped coach basketball. He dated the school athletic secretary Angie Allen. He married her in April 2048, and she did not even have to change her last name. They thought that was cool. He accepted a job at Hammonds Christian School that fall and was going to come home again. The family loved Angie, and was glad she was in the family.

Katie finished junior high in 2039 after one year. She was a real popular student and was homecoming queen and finished 4th in her class. She made many friends and dated a few boys. She won many talent shows and released 2 CDS and did some pageants as well. She helped many people and babysat and helped people in school and sports. She worked part time at a grocery store, and then at a local restaurant. She was a cashier at both jobs, and was an excellent hard worker. She played soccer and softball all 4 years. She was MVP of soccer as a junior and senior and set many school records. She was the softball MVP her senior year and was in many school plays and musicals. She graduated from high school in 2043.

She went to Hammonds Bible College and stayed there until 2047. She met many good friends. She married Jack Montgomery in September 2047. She played soccer all 4 years, and was co-captain her last 2 years, and MVP her last year. She graduated with honors and helped many people as well. She was very popular. She worked assisting the dean of women and residence life. She also worked as an admissions counselor her last 3 semesters. Her 1st 2 years she worked in the school cafeteria.

Megan was 4 when they moved there and 14 and a rising freshmen when her dad retired. She too could sing, but was a lot different than Katie .She could be wild, crazy, and like a boy at times. She was also more polite and quiet. She was a good singer as well, and loved to act. She was in the school and church plays and musicals. She watched her brother and sister play games, but never really got into sports. She was more feminine than her sister and aunt. She was very popular as well. She too helped others and encouraged many and made straight A's and always was very nice and courteous.

Meanwhile, Joe and Michelle were great. Joe loved preaching there. He had new preaching styles. Sometimes he could be charismatic. He would easily slip off his coat during sermons. Sometimes he dressed more casual. He opened the windows of the church and commanded loud singing so the neighbors could hear. He wanted the message of Jesus to get out.

He attended all of his kid's ball games. He cheered louder than anyone and was always the best fan. He won awards for that as well.

He challenged the people of the church. He dared them to get out and get more involved in the community and to help many. He told them to get out of comfort zones and to serve God wherever, however, and whenever. He asked people to go on mission field and attend Bible college no matter how old they were. He asked them to serve God and seek opportunities.

"We do not sit on the sidelines. The benchwarmers sit on the sidelines. I always played basketball and baseball and coached as well. There are always the best players and the not as good players. The best players get the time and the action, and the points. They are the leaders of the team and help the team win. They play a lot. The not as good players do not play as much. They do not score as much. They are valuable as well, and play, and score. But not as much, and they do not play so much.

"Do be the leaders. Do be the scorers. Get out on the court and score the points. Don't just sit there and say others will do it. You get out there and score the points and serve God and tell others of Him. Be a witness for God in all you say or do."

Joe worked well with the other staff members. The assistant pastor stayed for 4 years, and became a pastor in North Carolina. A new one started 6 months later, and he and Joe became close. As he was 30 and orphaned, Joe became a 2nd father to him. He would stay there 10 years. The youth director was there all 10 years as Joe. There was 3 children's director, 2 music directors, and 4 secretaries. Joe became close to them all and worked hard with them. He was an easy person to like.

Joe liked preaching on God's will. He encouraged many people to always seek God's will in all they did in their lives. He shared many stories on why you should seek God's will. He showed God's will is not always our will, and he has plans and changes for us we do not always see or want. Sometimes we do not want to go there or do this. Again, he talked about getting out of the comfort zone and doing things no matter what, even if we do not want to. He showed examples.

"In Oakley, there was a Baptist pastor named Artie Morris. He arrived there 2 years before me and retired there. He is my age. He had been in Martinez, West Virginia for 18 years. 3 of his 4 kids were born there and he loved it there. The church had seen his kids grow up, and one was married. He was not looking to move anywhere. He was not looking at other churches. He turned down 12 jobs in the past. They had a nice home. Oakley called twice and he always turned it down. He said he was happy and comfortable here. Family was close, and Oakley was 4 hours away. The house flooded one day and they had new carpets and the house looked nice. They also had 2 ceilings replaced. The house looked good for the market. The church asked him if he would be willing to move if it was God's will. He said of course. He preached 2 sermons there. He sent a sermon on disappointments and sadness to discourage him. They loved it, saying it touched their lives.

They read Experiencing God for church. They felt it was God's hand speaking to them. They finally accepted the job the third time they were asked and moved that summer after school year ended. They missed Martinez, but loved Oakley and the church and people a lot. They realized God's will and so should all of us."

Joe did much discipleship. He led courses and trained many people. He worked at camp a few more years and retired. He received many ovations and gifts for years of service. He taught evangelism courses, He helped college interns at the church. He helped students who attended the church. He visited the college and helped others as well. He attended the high school athletic events. He taught Bible studies and led worship at events. He preached at local events as well.

He wrote devotionals every year. He wrote a novel on a guy's life in the ministry. He wrote a children's book on a preacher's kid. He also wrote a book about a 56 year old preacher for 30 years who left to be a missionary to Korea for 8 years. They were all best sellers. The book about the missionary became a Christian movie, and then about the guy's life in the ministry.

The church grew more in the 10 years. It had 738 members when he left. There was 888 regulars every Sunday and 550 on Wednesday nights. A lot of college students attended, especially with the new 4 year college nearby and the growing economy. A new interstate, medical clinic, second mall, and 4 shopping centers were built in Hammonds. The city was growing as well. The Bible college had 1100 students, a new high. 3 new dorms, a chapel, 2 classroom buildings, and second gym had been built. The Christian school built 2 new dorms nearby for boarding students and built a new upper school classroom building and fine arts building. Hammonds was really growing. God was doing great things there.

Joe preached many sermons. He would stay on one Bible book for a while, and liked some subjects to talk on. He showed others to accept other people for who they are and do always love and accept them even if they did not fit in. He

151

preached on the elderly and to not forget them. He was getting that age himself. He encouraged them to go to nursing homes and see grandparents and older people and sit down and listen to their stories. He asked them to show them love.

He led community outreach projects. They worked in people's yards and did much good. They painted places. They repaired stuff damaged in storms. They worked for Habitat for Humanity, the local children's home, parks, the soup kitchen. They even helped out at other churches. They visited nursing homes and hospitals and did much good for people.

Joe and Michelle worked hard. She worked part time at the local Christian school. She subbed some as a teacher and secretary. She spent a year working at the music department at the Bible college. She released a CD of her singing. She wrote a couple of books on being a pastor's wife and being married to Joe with their different backgrounds. They were all best sellers. She was famous as well. Her parents died in 2044 a month apart, and she missed them, but knew they were in Heaven. She was happy to see her kids growing up, and saw 2 of them being married and getting a spouse.

Joe's mom Joey died in 2046. She was old and had lived a good life. She had served her Lord faithfully and was now in Heaven. The youth pastor preached her memorial service. The church was packed and around 200 people were standing up on the walls. She was 104.

The last year, stating in 2047, everyone knew he was going to retire the next year. He looked for a new pastor himself. Mike Martin was accepted and would arrive in May as a temporary associate pastor. Joe would retire in June, and Mike take over the next week. He was 48 and had been a missionary and pastor of a 200 member church in Taiwan for 12 years. Before that, he had been a pastor in Oklahoma for 6 years, and a youth director in 2 churches in Kansas before that.

Joe preached most every Sunday before that. He preached about missions and the need to spread God's word. He spoke about showing God to the world in actions and words. He showed how to do missions and tell of God no matter where

152

you are. He talked more of God's will and how to do know it. He led a Bible training course at the church 2 nights a week for 3 years. Many people got Bible training for free. He led an evangelism group that went out and ministered and witnessed to the community. In the 8 years he did this, 100 people in the area were saved. He started a new community Christian center near the church. He added on a new preschool/nursery wing and turned the old one into a bigger fellowship hall/lobby. He helped build a new Habitat for Humanity neighborhood for the poor and that was great.

He retired in June 2048 at the age of 70. He helped Mike for 3 weeks. He preached his final sermons. He would still attend the church in the years to come. He preached the nicest sermons. He would take a break for a while. He had a nice reception at the church. They were given nice presents and a big photo album for thanks for ministry. The church was packed. He had served God well here. And now he was ready for vacation and retirement.

Part Four: Retirement

Chapter 16
Retirement Years

Joe was now 70. He had worked hard past when most people retired. It was now 2048. They were looking forward to relaxing and spending time together. They wanted to travel. They had plans to go to places they had been before a long time ago. They planned to spend time with family and grand kids and friends. They were glad to be able to retire and do new things.

Joe was great at telling stories and keeping the grand kids entertained for hours. They loved hearing about the good old days and all that happened. His kids had enjoyed hearing them as well in the past. He was like Pa from Little House telling great stories. He told of old TV shows and movies and things that had happened to him in his lifetime. He warned them not to do a lot of the things he had done. He watched out for them, and showed them the way to follow God.

He told them of September 11, 2001. They had wanted to

know of someone that was around back then. "I was working that day 12-6. I was working as a computer technician. Susan and I were still living together for a few more weeks. I woke up at 8:00 and ran a couple of miles. I turned on the news at 8:47 at my house. The breaking news had just started. I could not believe what I was seeing. I could not believe what was happening. I yelled for Susan to come and watch. We watched in horror. I went to the bathroom around 9 and Susan was crying and screaming all of a sudden. She was yelling "It happened again. It happened again. It beeping happened again'. She added a few bad words as well. She yelled for me and I ran. It was so sad and shocking when we knew for sure it was on purpose. It was so sad when the towers fell and people were dying. It was a tough day. We learned America was not invincible. We pulled through somehow. We made it. We tried to be stronger. We saw heroes that day as well. It is a day we never will forget."

They had a next door neighbor named Margaret Dale. She was 70. She and her husband Preston had been married 34 years, but he had died 4 years before. She was a faithful member of the church and a good friend. They often checked on her and made sure she was ok. They fed her dog Beaudrot (Bo for short) when she went out of town. They loved her. She told great stories as well. She watched the houses when they and Lauren's families went places and helped them. They had been missionaries in Korea for 22 years and he had been a pastor for 17 years. They had worked together as people greeters at Wal Mart for 6 years and had been very popular. She ate with them once or twice a week.

Lauren's husband Mark died January 13, 2049 of pneumonia. He had lived a very good life. He was 76 and went to his reward. Many came to the funeral. Lauren and the kids and grand kids would miss him a lot, but were thankful for the love and memories and good years together. The assistant pastor spoke the funeral. Joe spoke as well. Mark had led a good full life and had served God faithfully for many years. Many people had been blessed through his ministry for years.

They and Lauren and some kids went on a long trip in the summer of 2049. They went to Asheville, North Carolina for 3 days. They went to Oakley, Virginia and stayed there for 3 nights and saw some old friends. They went to the Grand Canyon for 5 nights and the whole family was there. They then flew to Las Vegas and flew to Los Angeles for 5 nights and saw some movie and TV studios and Disney Land. Most of the family then went back home again. Joe, Michelle, Lauren and Naomi's family went to Kansas and stayed in Tyler for 4 nights. They then went to Walnut Grove for the Laura Ingalls festival. They were there 4 nights and De Smet for 2. They went to Mount Rushmore.

They stayed 3 nights in Ivy and 4 in Lansing. They went to Strawberry for 3 nights and finally to Monk for 3. There was still good friends around they loved and spent time with and enjoyed it very much. They enjoyed the trip and had a good time.

That October, Joe and Michelle visited England. They had a great trip and enjoyed many good things. They saw many great places they had read about for years. They met the Queen and the prime minister and some other famous people. They saw the great historic sites and loved Big Ben and Westminster Abbey and loved British accents and the beautiful countryside. They liked riding on other side of the car and the other side of the road. They rented a car and took tours. They saw some movies being made and watched a little.

Joe published his last update of his autobiography in February 2050. He chose retirement for his last update and was glad. It sold many copies. It was a much loved and treasured book and he mentioned many people he had known in his life.

Lauren went to be with the Lord in November 2050. She was 78, and she too had lived a full life serving her Jesus.

Many people came to the funeral, and she was mourned by the family, and again they were comforted by her life serving Jesus and the fact she was now in Heaven. She had helped many people and done a good ministry. She helped other pastor's wives and had served the churches well. She was missed by many. She was a leader for women in ministry.

Lauren's 3 kids and their families were good. Naomi was 52 and had 2 married kids, one was engaged, and she had one baby granddaughter and another on the way. Mark was 50 and both his kids were in college and in relationships. Suzanne was 46 and had one just married son and a daughter who was in college. They were doing well with stuff.

Michelle and Rebecca, his daughters, were 56 and grandparents for the first time. Joe was a great grandfather, and had a 16 year old daughter. Joe loved that fact and loved holding the babies. Michelle and Rebecca were both doing very well in life.

Luke was 46 and had one kid in high school and one ready to graduate college. Neither was in a relationship. Luke and his wife had worked through some issues and a trial separation and were now doing better than ever and working in insurance.

Adam was 28 had been married 2 years and had a new baby. He lived in the Atlanta area and worked for the Braves as a scout. He loved scouting the high schools and colleges. He sang at area churches and events and had a CD. He loved being a father.

Katie was 25, married and had a daughter. She worked part time in a grocery store in Monk. He worked at a pubic high school teaching math and teaching soccer. They lived in Joe's old neighborhood and the park was behind their house, and very popular. They met many interesting people in the area. They went on a car ride around the area every Sunday afternoon.

Megan was 20 and a student at Millwood Bible College in Pennsylvania. She dated a guy named Bryan. She worked on the yearbook staff and played intramural soccer. She made straight A's and enjoyed to sing. She had a CD as well.

February 2051 came quickly. Joe and Michelle went on a mission's trip to Germany for 10 days. They were not going to stop being active completely. They did evangelism work and saw 23 people come to Christ and 62 rededicate their lives. They loved seeing the historic places and many beautiful locations and sights. They had a great time. They also stopped by France for 5 days and Spain for 4. They loved Paris and Madrid and took in the sights and history.

Joe published his last book in November 2051. He was now 73. It was about God's will and prayer. It had many of his great stories in it. It was a best seller, like all the others. It had some poetry in it. He had published a children's book on the matter earlier that year. He also had written a youth edition that summer. All 3 were popular and used by many.

The 2050's went by good. More grandkids were born. Megan was married in 2056 to Tim Montgomery. His brother had married Katie. They had known each other almost all their lives and played in the nursery together as 4 and 5 year olds. By 2060, Adam had 3 kids and Katie 4 so Joe and Michelle had 7 grandkids together and they spoiled them all rotten.

They went on a trip every summer. In 2052, they spent a month in Florida. In 2053, they spent the whole summer in New York. In 2054, they spent 3 weeks in Strawberry and 2 in Texas. In 2055, it was Ohio for 3 weeks. They spent 2 months in Los Angeles in 2056, a month in Florida in 2057. They spent 4 weeks in Virginia in 2058, 2 weeks in Ivy in 2059. In 2060, they made one last trip. They spent 2 weeks at the Grand Canyon. Joe was 82 and was tired of traveling. Michelle was 65 and was ready to slow down as well. They had gone on a mission's trip to Honduras every spring from 2051-2057 but missions was now out as well. They were still in pretty good health and they got good exercise and stayed in shape. They loved listening to Christian radio shows and watching TV and reading together and driving every Sunday. They would drive through the college and then through the countryside and they always enjoyed that.

Joe still helped people and counseled them. He was still good on advice, and his mind was still very sharp. He read 1 book a week. People would come by and talk to him. He would sit on front porch and look out toward the road. People would come by and visit him. He went to town some. He still was in church every Sunday and helped some as well.

Joe loved the grandkids and great grand kids. He saw some a lot, and some only a few times a year. He told them all kinds of stories and jokes that had made him famous. Some were real, that happened to him and others. Some he made up.

He told them of his school days and wild days. They loved the stories of his days with Lauren. They all loved Lauren, and many wished they could have met her. They brought friends and they would gather around for his stories. They would be fascinated and listen intently and everyone loved him. He was Uncle Joe to so many people in town. He came to the ball games and pageants and plays and musicals and all the kids did and they loved for him to be there. He always cheered for them and supported them and cheered and clapped loud and they loved his support and love.

He told them the games they used to play. One time, they were playing Narnia and got on closet shelves and threw everything out on the floor, making a mess. Another time, they played hide and go seek and it took him 1 hour and 2 minutes to find her. The longest it took her to find him was 41 minutes. He told how they played with their neighbors Joe and Midge and played the greatest games. They had some other neighbors, an older couple named Michael and Melissa who provided candy and gum. This was in Carters. He talked about how strict Michelle's family was on Sundays.

Joe would tell them about the old television without pity site on the internet and the cool fun people who posted there. It was over 1200 pages and very popular. They made fun of Little House and all that went with it, especially Michael Landon. He posted as Halfpint, just like Laura's nickname. They showed a lot of stuff wrong with it. The kids loved hearing about this. They loved when Joe told of when the internet first came along and what it was like without it and before. They could not imagine life without it, especially since it was so awesome in 2061. It was the best ever.

They watched he old TV shows on DVD. They were good clean shows Joe had loved and they grew to love them as well. Joe still loved The Andy Griffith Show and Little House on the

162

Prairie the most after all these years. The kids laughed at the comedies. They loved The Three Stooges, Little Rascals, and The Honeymooners. Joe was glad the kids loved the show and loved hearing them laugh out loud. The shows were classics, and would always be loved by people.

Joe challenged them to video game tournaments. He could play good. But he and the parents did things right. They did not watch much TV. They walked and exercised a lot. They read and wrote a lot. Joe read books and stories to them. They loved to read as well. They loved the radio dramas Joe had collected and preserved. They listened to Odyssey for a long time and loved them all a lot. They had good manners and were polite and had learned from the best.

In 2061, soon after Megan had her 1st baby, Joe preached for the final time. There was a crusade in Hammonds. Shortly thereafter, he spoke 2 Sundays at the old church. He was glad to preach for some final times, and made it as great as always.

The crusade was Wednesday-Sunday. Joe spoke with some different preachers. He preached the sermon every night and helped lead an altar call. 32 were saved and 94 rededicated their lives. $ 89,000 was raised toward a new classroom building for the Bible college near the waterfall. Joe's teachings were very popular and people were moved by the testimonies.

Joe helped afterwards. When the pastor went to visit family for 2 weeks, he preached 2 Sundays. The family loved to hear him preach. He spoke eloquently and people listened intently. People enjoyed all he had to say and told him so after.

In 2062, Joe turned 84. He stopped walking after his birthday. He had a guest house built on the property. He hired a chauffeur. His grandson Matt brought groceries over every Saturday as he lived in the area. Joe and Michelle were really taking it easy. She retired from her 2 days a week at the restaurant. They stopped eating out and entertaining company for dinner. He stopped mailing out Bible lessons. They still entertained family. They did not cook as much.

Joe drank energy drinks. He still was in mostly good

health. He still had a sense of humor and played some jokes on the family. The friends of family would come by and visit him and they loved him. He had the craziest stories.

They would guess which was true and what he made up. He was loving retirement very much and was loving being able to relax a lot.

Chapter 17
Called Home to Heaven

Joe knew his life was coming to an end on earth. In 2063, he turned 85. He was not very active any more and pretty much stayed around the house and spent much time with the family. He went to church on Sundays and had other visitors as well. He read the Bible daily and loved reading other books. He also liked his old TV shows and listening to the radio.

They had a big party for him on June 1. The whole family and friends were in the church gym. Joe was very surprised and pleased and enjoyed himself very much. They gave him some good presents. He told his old stories. Everyone had a good time. They joked they could not put 85 candles on the cake, or it would be a mile long. They made some jokes about his age and everyone laughed. The kids made speeches for him and how much they loved him. Michelle spoke as well. The young grand kids played games and sang to him a song they had written. The song was a huge success.

Joe went to church one Sunday and saw his granddaughter Lisa singing a solo. During the sermon, he suddenly felt sick and had to leave the service. He was taken to the hospital overnight, but was feeling well again soon. He had enjoyed hearing Lisa sing very much. He was proud of her.

The family was concerned, and glad he was able to go home the very next day and they spent some time with him telling him stories about their lives and what was happening that week.

Christmas 2063 was great. The whole family gathered together for the holidays. They had a good time celebrating Jesus' birthday and talking of Him. They read Bible and prayed and sang songs and opened presents. They joked about Santa Claus and did some good stuff. They got some good presents and were very generous. They had some real good fellowship and it was nice.

The kids asked to hear about his first Christmas memory. Joe smiled. "My first Christmas memory was when I was 5years old. It was 1983. My favorite TV show was The Dukes of Hazzard. I got a Dukes lunch box and a General Lee car. I was so excited. I played with them non stop. I also got an Atlanta Braves hat, and a little jersey. I got $ 150, and that made me so happy. I had a cool spider toy and some Showbiz Pizza Place records. I loved listening to records back then. They were cool. My grandpa took me to the porch and had a good talk with me. We had a fun game of baseball in the backyard and played some board games. My sister and I entertained people with a puppet show, a contest, a fun board game, and some singing. She had some great presents as well. It was a good Christmas and I am glad I remember it. And of course, this is a good Christmas and I hope ya'll remember it and can one day tell your kids and grand kids about it."

Joe's mind was still very sharp. He had a good memory and could talk of great things. He could quote many Bible verses and even chapters as well. He could remember dates and events from the past very clearly and remembered the anniversaries.

Michelle was 68 and wrote her autobiography and it came out February 2064. It was a best seller and everyone loved it. They enjoyed hearing about the life from her perspective. She received many compliments and fan letters, just as Joe had done. They had a special P.O. Box for many years to receive the fan mail and the autograph requests from people. They had special pictures, and had personally autographed then to people. Now, he just signed his name and a Bible verse and sent them out to people. Michelle did some interviews from the home about the book and their lives.

A special video was made of his life. It came out in April and was a movie of his life. The whole family enjoyed it and it was very accurate. It touched on his childhood and bad years. It was mostly about his life in the ministry and marriage to Michelle. He had many good years in the ministry. The movie was well received and popular and received many good reviews. The kids loved seeing the movie. It was PG and had no real bad stuff in it as it was intended for whole families. It glossed over the bad stuff and just mentioned the problems and divorces and everything. The acting was very good and they were glad. The actors looked like them in some ways. Again, the interviews came and they were popular for a while. The actors came to Hammonds and they got together for a red carpet program as an extra on the movie. Joe and Michelle did some interviews and signed more autographs. And then they were ready to really slow down.

He had some dreams of Heaven. He said it was not as beautiful as it really is. The human mind cannot begin to imagine that. He had some dreams of his past and his family. He wrote some journals of how he was ready and loved his Lord.

Joe turned 86 that June. They were now leading private lives. They had signed over 1500 autographs and Adam handled sending them out now. He still read the letters and enjoyed them. They did no more interviews and he only went to church on Sundays. They hired a housekeeper, who was Margaret Dale's great-niece and she was great and helped a lot.

2064 was a good year. 2065 came. Joe knew it could be his last year on earth, and it was. He was still feeling healthy at the beginning of the year. His memory was slipping a little at times. He told some stories to help him. He spent time with all the kids.

In January 2065, He had the flu for 4 days and ran a high fever in July and was in the hospital for 4 nights. They considered putting him in a nursing home. A hospice nurse came to help out. He slipped and fell in February, but was not seriously hurt, and he walked with a walker. In March, he stayed in bed for the rest of his life. He had a TV with all the channels and video equipment and radio and CDs and audio cassettes. He had many books and was never bored. He turned 87 in June and they had a little celebration and the whole family came. The kids loved visiting his room.

In October, he had a virus and was hospitalized a few nights. They knew he was close to death and let him go home to bed and die. He would miss his family, and they would miss him but he was going to Heaven and would be healthy again.

Rebecca and daughter Michelle were 71. Their grandchildren were growing up and in college.

One had a baby, to make Joe a great great grandfather. Luke was 61 and had 5 grandkids and his kids were grown and living in Alabama and working.

Adam was 43 and his kids were good. Mark was 15, Lisa 13, and Mike 9. They lived in Marshall, near Michelle's family, and it was just a hour and a half away. He now worked at Wal Mart and his wife at a grocery store. Mark worked Saturdays bussing tables at a local restaurant. Lisa was in 8th grade and played soccer. Mike played baseball with his friends a lot, and was getting very good. Adam taught Sunday school and helped in the youth department at church.

Katie was 41. She still looked great. Lauren was 15 and learning to drive and babysitting. Chris was 11 and now in junior high and had his first girlfriend. Luke was 8, and loving 3rd grade. Cathy was 5 and in K-5 and learning a lot. She had a great memory and memorized Bible verses. She had the best manners ever and all the adults loved her and helped people in big ways. She was very mature for her age. She was a good singer as well and had many friends. Jack worked in insurance and Katie worked at a local church and Habitat for Humanity restore and she loved them both and was good at it. They lived in Montgomery, 27 minutes from Hammonds and were able to visit a lot and that is why they were close.

Megan was good with Tim. Tim and Jack were brothers, as they were sisters. They lived in Hammonds down the street from Joe. They worked in real estate. Ed was 4 and Lindsay 9 months. Megan was 35 and helped at the soup kitchen some and the people loved her. The kids loved drama and did skits and puppet shows and the family loved them very much.

On October 13, it became clear that Joe would die that day. It was a Tuesday morning and the whole family gathered at the house. The last ones arrived right before noon. They were excused from work for the day of course.

They all spent time in Joe's room and he was alert most of the time. He closed his eyes a lot. He was very weak and had a fever. The nurse and a doctor were there. They helped him when they could. He smiled a lot as they talked to him.

Joe told some jokes. He told some funny stories of people he knew over the years. They looked at photo albums and watched some old home videos all afternoon. Joe talked to the little families separately. They had some good moments together and laughed and cried. He told them special memories of each one and told them of their talents and how much they meant to him. They told him how much they loved him and the special things he did for them and how much they loved him. They sang some. He saw their little skits. The kids would read out of a book to him.

At 7:00 Joe closed his eyes a lot more. He was feeling very weak and knew the time had come to meet his Jesus.

They all came in and kissed and hugged him and exchanged "I love you's." All the grand kids and great grandkids went to the main house. Michelle and the 6 kids and spouses remained. He told them of the memorial service and all that would happen. He told them how he wanted things and how they could handle things. They nodded and promised to carry out his wishes.

The spouses left and went to the main rooms. The children spent 20 minutes with him and they laughed and cried and hugged and kissed and held his hands. They all shared special memories. They all loved him and said "See you later" and went across the hall.

Michelle was with him at the end at 7:47 PM. She was holding his hand and talking to him. He had his eyes closed and nodded some. They kissed on lips. They said goodbyes and I love you. His breathing stopped and he went home to be with His Lord.

The family gathered around and the men came in and took him to the funeral home. They cried some because they would miss him on earth. But he was in a much better place and was with Jesus in Heaven and was pain free and healthy. He had lived a full good life and had many fine years of ministry. He had served his Jesus well. He always said he was saved by grace, and was thankful God had chosen a man like him to serve Him. He had made an impact in many lives, and had gone to his reward.

The wake was held Thursday night the 15th at the funeral home. Many people gathered and it was a nice evening considering. Many people shared memories and how much he meant to them and how much they loved him and they knew he had loved them. They shared how much he had helped them and shown them and taught them new things.

The memorial service was packed Friday the 16th. People gathered in the fellowship hall and classroom to watch on video. The sanctuary was packed. Many people gathered to show their love and support. They showed love to the family.

The preacher preached the sermon. The kids and Michelle shared eulogies. So did some friends. There was much laughter and tears. They shared some funny memories of him and all the stuff he used to do. They talked of his practical jokes and pranks he was famous for back in the day. He made funny

170

phone calls and the funniest email messages. They showed how much he loved his family and helped them. He was a great family man and spoiled them rotten at times. He showed them Christ's love and how to act and respect and how to know God and love Him. He showed them what not to do. He taught them the right path in life and read the Bible and prayed with them a lot and prayed for them.

The pastor spoke. "Joe never felt worthy of all this. He considered himself "saved by grace." He felt he was the worst of sinners with a lot of stuff he did in his life. He knew he was a sinner and had messed up in some big ways. He never felt he was worthy of being famous and all the attention and autographs and movies. He felt inadequate at times. But he loved his God and lived his whole life after salivation for Him. He gave his heart and soul and whole life to the ministry serving God.

"Joe loved his family so much. He was always teaching them new and interesting things. He brought home little presents and trinkets. He taught them to be the best little people and how to respect others and have good manners. They had the utmost respect for elders and were loved. They were obedient and grew up to be fine Christians and help their families and raise them to be good Christians and they are all good. Joe was a good role model for the family and it shows.

"Joe had a great ministry. He touched many lives. His sermons were very interesting and kept people paying close attention. Many people were touched and were saved. He had the greatest stories and jokes. He helped many people and gave much advice and encouragement. He had a helping hand for many. He was the nicest kindest man possible. His books were great and many people enjoyed them. He always followed God's will and wanted to serve God in many ways and was willing to go wherever God called him. He served the schools and churches very well and helped so many people.

"Joe Allen lived a full life. He served his Lord faithfully. He never wavered. He stayed true to the end. We should follow his examples and follow Jesus in all we do. Never give up.

Encourage others. Seek God's will. Teach others of Jesus. Tell others of Him. Be missionaries no matter where you are. Follow Joe's example and serve God all in your lives."

The family had a big reception. Many people shared memories of Joe. There was a good and sad time remembering Joe. He was well loved. Sympathy notes piled in from all over the country and world. Joe had touched many lives. People sent thank you notes as well. The family was touched by the love. They were thankful for the many years with Joe.

Joe was now In Heaven for all eternity. He was with his Jesus. He had begun a life that would never end. Joe Allen would be with His Lord forever.

Printed in the United States
90011LV00002B/229-231/A